Dr. York and the Pocket Watch

MAVIS E. MADISON, JR. MYSTERY

BOOK ONE

A. Genea Seymour

Mavis E. Madison, Jr.

Dr. York & the Pocket Watch

iii

Veritas et Virtus

Thomas-Scott Academy
1922

DEDICATION

To the three most important women in my life — **my mother, Mavis; my maternal grandmother, Evelyn; and my daughter Madison.** My admiration and love for you three is immeasurable — your love, strength, and legacy live in every page of this story. **To my dad, Gregory** – who when I asked to go to boarding school, he did not hesitate, thank you dad. Also, to all my young readers who believe in adventure — *Mavis E. Madison, Jr.,* is here to take you on a journey filled with curiosity, courage, and fun. May this first book of the series spark your imagination and remind you that mystery lives in the heart of those brave enough to seek it.

Table of Contents

Administrators & Chaplain

Headmistress Wednesday Menard

Deputy Headmaster Aian Ying

Dean Alejandra French

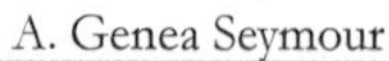

Father Dyan Trent

STUDENTS

Mavis Evelyn Madison, Jr.

Willow Spelman

Cynthia Brice

Toppy Li

Princess Francis

Edward Loftus Farrington

Kimp Jackson

Pierson Lockwood

Axton Stevenson

CHAPTER 1 - ORIENTATION

Mavis stood on the veranda of the administration building, flanked by her parents. Her mother was mid-chatter with two other families, proudly recounting how she and her older daughters had attended Thomas-Scott Academy—and now, with great honour, her youngest was enrolled. Mavis rolled her eyes so hard she feared they might get stuck. Everyone was boasting about who they were and where they came from. She was already over it.

"Mavis Evelyn Madison, Jr.," called a full-figured woman with a distracting mole bouncing on her upper lip as she spoke. Her voice sliced through the crowd like a bell.

Mavis and her parents approached the table. The woman sat in a wooden chair that looked as uncomfortable as her expression.

Mavis leaned in, her palms flat on the table. Their faces were almost too close. "May you please refer to me as Madison?" she asked politely.

The woman glanced between Mavis and her parents, then back at the roster. Her chipped nail polish tapped the page. "The roster says Mavis Evelyn Madison, Jr.—not the reverse."

Mrs. Madison stepped in smoothly. "We have no problem with you calling her Madison," she said with a smile, while her husband stood silently, holding his breath. He knew his wife's poise could shift to abrasiveness if provoked.

The woman nodded, checked off Mavis' name, handed her a nametag, and immediately called the next student—without so much as a response. Mrs. Madison blinked, stunned by the dismissiveness. This wasn't the behavior she remembered from her alma mater. She waited behind as her husband and daughter entered the auditorium. Once the family ahead had moved on, and the woman called the next student, Mrs. Madison stepped forward.

"Was that necessary?" she asked, voice calm but firm. The woman looked perplexed, clearly not thinking twice about the Madisons. "You were dismissive to my daughter's request, and you ignored me completely."

The woman glanced at the growing line of parents and offered a hollow apology. "It's a hectic day—just trying to get everyone tagged and inside for orientation." She tilted her head and beckoned the next family forward.

Mrs. Madison shook her head, annoyed. The apology was empty, and she knew it. But this was Mavis' first day. She wouldn't sour the moment by unleashing her less pleasant side. Not today.

"Why did you stay behind?" her husband asked, handing her a booklet.

"I wanted her to understand that she was rude, and we won't accept it."

"So, what did she say?"

Mrs. Madison sucked her teeth. "That woman is rude by nature." She fanned her hand in the air, still simmering.

Inside, the auditorium buzzed with chatter and the scraping of chairs across polished oak floors. Students and parents clustered together, eager to sit beside familiar faces. At the podium stood Headmistress Wednesday Menard, waiting for the last few to settle. She looked like a no-nonsense woman— about 5'7", hair tightly wound in an upswept bun, platform black shoes, and a pale blue floral dress cinched at the waist with a slender black belt. Fashion week had clearly skipped her, Mavis thought, stifling a laugh. She scanned the crowd for her roommate, Cynthia Brice, but no one nearby wore a nametag with that name.

"Okay everyone, let's get settled in," Headmistress Menard said, clapping her hands and surveying the room.

Mrs. Madison sat with pride, admiring the portraits of the school's founders and distinguished alumni. The panel of administrators took their seats. Students and parents were finally settled. Orientation could begin.

"I'd like to welcome you all to Thomas-Scott Academy," Headmistress Menard began. "We have a long history of excellence. This year marks our centennial celebration. A grand ball will be held on June 25th, 202, so you'll have plenty of time to prepare your attire. It will be a year of exciting events." She paused, then continued with a firmer tone. "We are a co-ed institution with strong values of success and respect. Boys and girls attend classes together, and we offer both co-ed and separate extracurricular activities. We expect you to uphold the standards of our school."

She gestured to Mr. Ying, the Deputy Headmaster, who rose and joined her at the podium. He was stern—so much so that even his white moustache seemed stiff, curled at the tips like it had been starched.

"Another school year is upon us," he said. "We aim to remain the envy of every school in the region. As Headmistress Menard mentioned, this is a special year. We play hard, but we work harder. Right?" He nodded, answering his own question. "Now, I'll turn things over to our Chaplain, Father Trent, who will lead us in devotion."

Father Trent was the first to smile. He stepped up to the podium. "All heads bowed, and eyes closed," he instructed. Everyone complied. He offered a prayer and welcomed the students to Thomas-Scott Academy.

Then came Mrs. French, the Dean. She smiled warmly as she approached the podium. "Look at all of you," she said, arms outstretched. "New faces, ready to begin your journey. We look forward to nurturing the best in each of you. This campus spans 150 acres—there's so much to explore. We encourage you to get familiar with your new home." Her tone shifted. "That said, you are not permitted to enter the abandoned antique and pawn shop at the western edge of campus. It's been closed for over fifty years and is not affiliated with the school. We don't want anyone getting hurt."

She pointed into the crowd, her eyes scanning for troublemakers.

Mavis' curiosity ignited. Her mother's warning glance was immediate. She knew her daughter's mind had already twisted "keep out" into "go explore." Mavis swallowed and looked away.

"Mavis..." her mother leaned in.

"Yes, ma'am," she replied, bracing for the speech.

"You heard Dean French. I have nothing else to add."

"Yes, ma'am." Mavis nodded obediently, but the words had already slipped out her left ear and tumbled off a cliff. She was going to check that place out. No question.

She smiled sweetly at her mother.

"Good girl," Mrs. Madison said, turning her attention back to Headmistress Menard, who was now sharing housekeeping details.

Chapter 2 – Fast Friends

Mavis was anxious to get upstairs to her room. She'd been assigned to Ferguson-Redd, the same dorm her sister Patricia had once called home. Patricia had spoken fondly of the courtyard and the whispered stories of students sneaking about after hours. Mavis was relieved to be the first to arrive—she wanted the bed closest to the window.

She clapped her hands as she opened the door. "Yippee! I get the bed near the window!"

Mr. Madison followed with two trunks, and Mrs. Madison carried a duffel bag. Mavis, with her green leather backpack slung over one shoulder, rushed to the window. The courtyard below was exactly as Patricia had described—four royal poinciana trees at each corner, eight wooden benches, and a majestic sapodilla tree standing proudly in the center. Her father joined her at the window, admiring the view. Her mother, meanwhile, tested the mattress with few firm bounces of her hand. Thirty minutes later, Cynthia Brice and her family arrived, buzzing with excitement. Mrs. Madison sprang into action, introducing herself with practiced charm as Mr. Brice struggled in with the bags. Mrs. Brice was equally chirpy, hugging Mrs. Madison like they were old friends.

"So, our girls will be rooming together," Mrs. Brice said, smiling at Cynthia and then at Mavis.

Cynthia's younger brother Timothy was a whirlwind— opening drawers, sliding closet doors back and forth, and exploring every corner.

"Stop that, Tim," his father scolded, though the boy paid no mind. "Please excuse him," he added. "He's a busy seven-year-old."

Mr. Madison chuckled. "We know what that's like. Our Mavis was just as active at his age."

"Dad," Mavis groaned, mortified.

Mr. Brice finally caught hold of Timothy. "Tim, don't forget your manners. Say good afternoon to the Madisons."

"Afternoon," Timothy mumbled, eyes already scanning for his next distraction.

"Are these your only children?" Mrs. Madison asked.

"No, Timothy's the last of seven," Mrs. Brice replied proudly.

Mrs. Madison's eyes widened. "Good heavens, that's a house full. I'm tired just thinking about all that talking and scolding."

Mrs. Brice laughed. "It was a time, but thank God Cyn is here, and now we only have Timothy to contend with."

Meanwhile, Cynthia and Mavis stood by the window, getting acquainted. Mr. Madison smiled, pleased to see his daughter settling in.

"I hope you don't mind that I took the window side," Mavis said.

"Oh, not at all. I would've picked the bed near the bathroom anyway."

"Great! Are you from Madlemor?"

"No, we're from Spikenard Island."

"Oh, my goodness, that place is gorgeous! I've never been, but I've seen photos. I'd love to visit."

"Well, consider yourself invited—any holiday you choose."

"Geez, thanks!" Mavis beamed. "Mum, guess where Cynthia is from?"

Mrs. Madison guessed everywhere but the right place.

"She's from Spikenard Island!"

"That's spectacular. We've been meaning to vacation there but haven't had the chance. Now we have no excuse—our daughters are friends," she said, nudging her husband.

He nodded in agreement.

"So, where are you all from?" Mr. Brice asked, mounting a 25" flatscreen on Cynthia's side of the room. Mr. Madison helped him steady it.

"Coco Plum Cay," Mrs. Madison replied.

"You're far from home—what is that, 1800 miles or more?" Mr. Brice said, now helping his wife hang Cynthia's clothes in the shared closet.

"Indeed. But it's tradition. I attended this school, and so did my girls. I'm originally from Madlemor—southern side—but haven't had reason to return except when my daughters are enrolled."

"Nice. How was it back then?" Mrs. Brice asked, intrigued.

"I loved it. I was an only child, and suddenly I had sisters everywhere. My girls loved it too, and now my Mavis will follow suit."

"Mum—Madison, please," Mavis begged.

The Brice's looked confused.

Mrs. Madison smiled. "Yes, dear. She prefers Madison instead of Mavis."

"Mavis is such a beautiful name," Mrs. Brice said.

"I agree—it's my first name. But she dislikes being a junior."

"It's an honour to share your mother's name," Mrs. Brice added warmly.

Mavis felt that familiar mix of embarrassment and frustration tighten around her throat. Was it so wrong to want her own name? She thought to herself, smiling politely.

"I'll call you Madison," Cynthia said.

"Thank you," Mavis whispered.

Timothy darted down the hallway just as Mr. Brice opened the door to empty the trash. "Timothy, stop running!" he called. Ms. Biggertoe, the housemother, stepped out of her room. "He's an active one, isn't he?" she said, smiling as Timothy zoomed past with his arms outstretched like airplane wings.

Mr. Brice caught him mid-flight. "Okay, Captain—time to land."

Ms. Biggertoe chuckled and leaned against her doorframe as they returned to the room.

"Everything's put away. Time to say our 'until we see you soon,'" Mrs. Madison said. "Sweetie, come kiss-kiss." Her lips were already puckered. "And remember what I told you earlier— no sleuthing, snooping, or curious hobbies."

Mavis hugged her tightly. "Mum, no worries. I'll be on my best behavior."

"Take care of yourself and Cynthia," her dad added, kissing her forehead.

"I shall, Dad."

"We better head out," Mr. Brice said. "Tim needs lunch, and we need to rest before our flight tonight."

"Safe travels," Mr. Madison said.

Cynthia walked her family to the elevator. She would miss home, but like Mavis, she'd dreamed of coming here for as long as she could remember. Back at the room door, she quickly wiped away tears before turning the knob.

"So... what shall we do now? Lunch is at noon, and we've got two hours before we need to be assembled and on our best behavior," Mavis said.

Cynthia pursed her lips, shrugging her shoulders. "I don't know. What do you have in mind?"

Mavis grabbed both her hands and pulled her to the window. "I was thinking we could go on an adventure... and check out that antique and pawn shop."

Cynthia gasped. "Are you nuts? That's the one place that's off-limits! Remember Adam and Eve? They ate from the tree of knowledge and got banished from Eden!"

"Why are we having a Bible story?"

"My point is—we could be banished. Expelled, Madison. Expelled."

Mavis tapped her shoulder. "We won't be banished," she said, laughing. "We're just looking around. That's all."

"Yeah, looking around for trouble," Cynthia muttered.

A knock interrupted them.

"Have you made new friends?" Mavis asked.

"Nope. Thought it was for you."

The knock came again.

Cynthia opened the door.

A smiling girl greeted them. "I'm Willow. Willow Spelman. One of your suitemates."

"Oh, come in," Mavis said. Cynthia opened the door wider.

"I saw you on the line, Mavis. That lady was so rude to you and your mum."

Mavis smiled. "Yes—the mole lady."

Willow laughed. "Right? So, distracting."

"Anyway, please call me Madison. And this is my roommate, Cynthia."

"Cyn," she said. "Just call me Cyn. Not 'sin'—'C-y-n.'"

Mavis snorted. "You're so silly. Cyn, not sin."

"We should sit together at lunch," Willow offered.

"Is your roommate here yet?" Mavis asked.

"No, she's coming tomorrow. There was a delay, Ms. Biggertoe said."

"Oh...." Mavis replied.

Willow took the seat closest to the door—Cynthia's chair. Cynthia was relieved Willow had interrupted Mavis' bright idea of exploring the antique and pawn shop.

She sat on her bed, and Mavis joined her.

"I've heard so much about this academy. I love that it's co-ed," Willow said, admiring the room. "Nice—you have two TVs. How will you decide which to watch?"

"We can watch both, just keep the volumes low," Cynthia explained.

"My last school was all girls. It's nice to have a mix."

"You did primary school away from home?" Cynthia asked, shocked.

"I've been in boarding school since fourth grade. My parents travel a lot, and my older siblings from my dad's first marriage are adults. So, it's just me—life as an only child."

"That must've been awful," Mavis said sympathetically.

"Nah, it was great—having so many friends and doing fun things. It wasn't far from home; it was only a two-hour drive, so I went home some weekends and most holidays," she said.

"Interesting," Cynthia said. "I would hate to have been away from my family so early, but if it worked for you, then who are we to judge?"

"Anyway, girls, I am starving. Let's get to the dining hall before all the food is devoured."

Mavis looked at Cynthia and could see the relief on her face—they were going to lunch instead of snooping around the antique and pawn shop.

Chapter 3 – The Introductions

"It smells so delicious—whatever they've fixed," Willow said, inhaling deeply as they stood in line outside the dining hall.

The line was long, and it was only for first-year students. They could only imagine the chaos once the full student body arrived.

"Yeah, it does. My stomach's hollow—I can hear the echo of it screaming for food," Cynthia groaned.

They all laughed.

"Hey, watch it!" Mavis snapped, jolted forward by a bump from behind. She turned to see a boy with a sheepish smile.

"My apologies. I'm Elf," he said, extending a slender hand.

Mavis frowned and didn't take it. "Okay, Elf. Just be careful next time," she said, turning back toward the entrance.

"No introduction?" he asked, sounding disappointed.

She gave him a look. "You bumped me, you apologized, I accepted. Now keep it moving."

The line inched forward, to everyone's relief. Elf stood silently behind her.

"Do we just sit anywhere?" Cynthia asked as a girl at the door welcomed them inside.

"Only for this weekend. Your table assignments will be posted on your floor by this evening."

"Great. Table assignments," Mavis mumbled.

Inside, the buffet line was a feast—cracked conch, grouper fingers, mounds of fries, chicken souse, sheep tongue souse, baked macaroni, curry chicken, white rice, and trays of mangoes and pineapples.

"So much food—and it smells amazing," Willow said.

Mavis, a curry-chicken enthusiast, grabbed a bowl with steaming white rice. Cynthia, ravenous, loaded her plate with grouper fingers, peas and rice, and a bowl of sheep tongue souse. Willow, indecisive and enthusiastic, sampled nearly everything—chicken and sheep tongue souse, peas and rice, and a bowl of fruit.

"Young lady, are you preparing for hibernation?" Headmistress Menard asked dryly, eyeing Willow's towering tray.

"Hibernation?" Willow mouthed to the girls, confused. She turned around, flustered. "Ah, no, ma'am."

"My dear, you can come up for seconds. We don't charge by the plate here," Menard said, her tone laced with sarcasm.

Willow laughed nervously. "Yes, ma'am."

"Eat slowly—you don't want gas. Mrs. Finkle and her staff will be pleased to know they've found a new fan."

The girls found seats near the window with a view of the veranda.

"Hey, girls," a voice with a strong southern accent called out. "I'm Princess Francis, but everyone back home calls me Franny. May I join y'all?"

"Sure," Mavis said, catching her breath between bites.

"So, where's everyone from?" Franny asked, settling beside Cynthia.

"I'm from Coco Plum Cay," Mavis said. "And she's from Spikenard Island," she added, pointing to Cynthia.

"And you?" Franny asked Willow.

"Guinep Cay," Willow replied between bites.

"Guinep Cay—wow! My family goes there every year to visit my granny. My mum's Guineptian."

"Nice," Willow said, returning to her food.

"This place is so exciting. I've heard so much about it," Franny said, speaking at a speed of 100 miles per second.

The girls smiled, nodding as they continued eating.

"May we sit?" Elf and three other boys stood nearby with trays in hand.

"Sure," Franny said.

"I'm Axton Stevenson," said a boy of modest frame; his voice surged like a river in a flood. "This is Pierson Lockwood," he added, gesturing to a boy with metal braces that gleamed like mirrors. "And he's Kimp Jackson," he said, pointing to the last boy—average height, wavy blonde hair, hazel-green eyes, and dimples that deepened as he smiled.

"I'm Elf," Elf added, leaning forward since Axton had skipped him—tiny frame, big dark brown curls, easy to overlook.

"Elf?" Franny repeated, smiling.

"Yip."

"That's different," she said, waiting for an explanation that never came.

A glass clinked at the head table. Headmistress Menard stood.

"I hope you're all enjoying lunch. Dinner will be served at six. Your official tables will be listed on your floors. Starting Monday, boys will eat on the left side of the dining hall, girls on the right. Enjoy the rest of your lunch."

"Drats. We can't sit where we want," Axton groaned. "What's the point of being co-ed if we're separated?"

"I agree," Franny said.

"We have classes together," Willow offered.

"Are we sure of that?" Kimp asked. "We all thought we could eat wherever we wanted—until now. Let's wait for the first day of classes before assuming."

Willow shrugged and returned to her food.

Chapter 4 – Brown Paper Bag & Starch

"What on earth are you doing?" Mavis asked, glancing up from a fashion magazine at her desk and eyeing Cynthia with raised brows.

"I'm ironing," Cynthia replied smartly. "What does it look like I'm doing?" she added with a sarcastic twist.

Mavis slung her arm over the back of her chair. "Well, you've got a torn paper bag resting on your skirt, so I was thinking maybe you're trying to start a fire. Is this some kind of escape plan?"

Cynthia rolled her eyes. "No, silly. Haven't you ever ironed with a brown paper bag and starch before?"

"Starch, yes. Brown paper bag, no," Mavis said, laughing.

"Watch and learn, little mouse. The brown paper bag helps lay the pleats in place. The steam on the bag makes them neat and stiff with the starch—perfect combo. Old school, I tell you. It's classic," Cynthia boasted.

Mavis burst out laughing. "You're a riot. I've never seen that done before, but I'm intrigued. Iron on, my expert dry cleaner."

Cynthia grinned. "I *am* an expert."

She returned to her task, and Mavis watched in awe at the precision Cynthia gave each pleat. And this was just the first of five plaid skirts—red and navy blue. *This will take forever*, Mavis thought.

"All done! First of five!" Cynthia declared like she'd won a medal.

Mavis was genuinely impressed. The pleats lay perfectly, as if cemented in place. "You can iron for me. My skirts look nowhere near that pressed. I just run the hot iron across them and hope for the best."

"I love being neat, and I love ironing. So sure—I'll iron your skirts. In exchange, I'll find something for you to do for me."

"Bring it on. I'm sure I've got skills you can use."

"I've got four more skirts and five collared shirts to go, so I better get on it."

"All done. If you did it my way—poof, pow, like magic—you'd be finished already."

Cynthia laughed. "Nope. I'm good my way."

Chapter 5 – First Day

Mavis didn't sleep much. The anxiety of starting her first day of classes had her tossing and turning all night. Cynthia, on the other hand, slept soundly—unbothered and peaceful—when Mavis glanced over at her around 4 a.m. She rolled onto her side and began counting the seashells printed on her pale blue Androsia drapes, gently swaying in the cool early morning breeze. Just as she drifted into a second sleep, her alarm screamed from the side table. She swatted it like a fly, sending it clattering to the floor. Thankfully, it was made of hard plastic and well-acquainted with abuse. The crash jolted Cynthia awake. Mavis was already on her knees, saying her morning prayers. Cynthia followed suit without hesitation. They finished at the same time.

"First day!" Mavis said, clapping as she rose from beside her bed.

Cynthia stretched, then dropped to the floor for a few quick exercises before rummaging through her drawer for a satin slip, camisole, and other essentials. Mavis was already in the shower. Toppy Li, one of their suitemates, knocked on the bathroom door to let Mavis know she was waiting. She'd arrived late the night before, and they hadn't met her yet.

Cynthia turned her desk chair toward the full-length mirror on the door. She ran her fingers through her thick, shoulder-length dusty brown braids, and parted them neatly down the center. She plaited each side and secured the ends with black rubber bands.

Mavis knocked on the door when she was done, keeping her promise to alert Toppy. She'd brushed her teeth in the shower and returned to the room with her caddy. From behind the closed door, Toppy shouted a cheerful "Thank you!"

"We need a shower schedule for mornings," Cynthia said.

"Yup. Suitemate meeting," Mavis replied.

Cynthia waited for Willow to finish in the bathroom before heading in herself—she didn't like rushed showers. By the time she emerged, Mavis was already dressed, her thick, kinky dark brown curls bouncing past her shoulders.

"Aren't you going to do something with your hair?" Cynthia asked, rubbing vanilla and chamomile lotion into her arms.

Mavis fluffed her curls. "What's wrong with my hair?"

"It's not combed. That's what's wrong with it," Cynthia said, deadpan.

"There's nothing wrong with it. See. It's bouncy." She bounced it like a basketball.

Cynthia glanced at the clock. "We've got time. Come here." She pulled Mavis to the mirror and began raking a comb through her hair from root to tip. "This hair is not cleared out. Why don't you take better care of your crown?" she scolded, sounding decades older than her age. "I'll put it in one for today, but when we get back, I'm plaiting it."

"Plait?" Mavis echoed.

"Yes, plait. Don't you ever plait it? Or your mummy?"

"Nope. My mother is not the plaiting type. You saw her—her hair's just as free as mine."

Cynthia laughed. "I didn't pay much attention. But see! All done." She stepped back. "Your hair's so beautiful... and yet so unloved."

Mavis rolled her eyes. "I guess so. Can we go now?"

"Ah—what's that around your neck?" Cynthia pointed with her left index finger.

"What are you, my warden?"

"Nope. But seriously, what is that?"

"It's my tamarind seed pearl necklace. My grandmother made it for me."

"You know Headmistress Menard isn't going to let you wear that thing."

"We'll just see about that, warden," Mavis said, shaking her head sassily.

Chapter 6 – The Tamarind Seed Necklace

The auditorium was packed to the brim. The noise level could've raised the roof—chairs screeched across the floor, voices ricocheted from corner to corner, and the air buzzed with first-day excitement. Mavis and Cynthia walked arm in arm, giddy to begin their classes. The vaulted wooden ceilings loomed above, bamboo ceiling fans spinning at full speed. Canary yellow walls, trimmed with white crown molding and baseboards, framed the room like a cheerful postcard. Near the stage hung a gold antique-framed photograph of Mrs. Wilhelmina Thomas-Scott, the academy's founder and heiress. She had believed fiercely in the power of education for all. In the photo, she stood beside her two children—a son and a daughter—handsome and poised.

Mavis paused, admiring the family's elegance.

"Mavis Evelyn Madison, Jr.," a voice boomed, bouncing off the walls and landing smack-dab in her ear. She nearly stumbled.

"What have I done?" she whispered to Cynthia, who shrugged, equally confused.

The room fell silent. Great, Mavis thought. Now everyone knows my full name.

Headmistress Menard stood before them, stern and unyielding. "Young lady why are you wearing that dreadful seeded, beaded necklace?" she asked, pointing at Mavis' tamarind seed pearls.

Mavis instinctively touched her neck, shielding the necklace. "I always wear pearls, Headmistress Menard."

"Not during school hours. It's not part of the dress code," she snapped. "Take them off. Now." She held out her hand.

Mavis unclasped the necklace, her fingers trembling. "May I please keep it? I won't wear it during school again."

"Fine. But if I see it again, it's mine until the end of the school year—and that's June," Menard said, turning sharply and walking away.

All eyes were on Mavis. Her cheeks burned with embarrassment. Menard resumed directing students—boys to the right, girls to the left.

"I told you not to wear that thing," Cynthia whispered as they took the first two seats on the left side of the room.

"I know, I know. But I didn't think it'd be a big deal," Mavis murmured.

"So now you won't wear it anymore, right?"

"Girl, please. I'll just wear it under my shirt."

"Madison," Cynthia hissed through gritted teeth.

"Don't worry, my dearest warden. I'll be fine. She won't see it."

"I'm still shaking. That woman is vicious," Cynthia said, crossing her ankles. Mavis fiddled with the necklace in her skirt pocket, her fingers curling around the familiar beads.

Father Trent stepped forward to lead the opening prayer. Deputy Headmaster Ying stood beside him, and as soon as the final "Amen" echoed through the room, Ying began his welcome speech.

"Today marks the beginning of a new academic year. We expect excellence, respect, and dedication from each of you. Work hard, and you'll thrive. Now let us all rise to sing the school song," he announced.

"I don't know the school song," Cynthia whispered.

"Neither do I," Mavis admitted. "They sent it in the summer packet, but I didn't think we'd sing it this early. I've heard it a million times from my mum and sisters, and still—I don't know it. I've got a trick," she added. "Learned it in my junior church choir."

"You sing in a choir?" Cynthia asked, surprised.

"Yes. So, listen—just mime 'winter weather.' It looks like you know the words."

Cynthia looked skeptical. "You're kidding, right?"

"Nope. Just go along. You'll see."

With nothing to lose, Cynthia followed her lead. They mouthed "winter weather" with gusto, like seasoned performers. It worked. No one noticed.

They giggled behind cupped hands as they sat down.

"See," Mavis whispered.

"You were right," Cynthia replied, grinning.

Chapter 7 – Elf

"Madison," she heard as she walked to her locker. She turned around.

"Hey, Willow," she said, stopping to let her catch up.

"This is Toppy Li," Willow said, introducing their other suitemate.

"So, you were the one rushing me out of the shower this morning," Mavis teased.

"I'm sorry—I like to shower early. Maybe we can agree on a schedule for the four of us, so we don't interrupt each other."

"Sure," Mavis replied. "I was thinking we needed a suitemate meeting."

"Not a bad idea. Let us know when," Toppy agreed.

"Will do."

"Anyway, we better get to class. I don't want Menard shouting at us like she did you earlier," Willow said.

"I know, right? All because of my pearls."

They parted ways. Mavis grabbed her books for her first three classes and stuffed them into her backpack. Literature was her first subject. She loved reading—not the mushy fluff, but murder mysteries and suspense. She knew this class wouldn't be that kind, but she was excited, nonetheless. She could devour a two-hundred-page novel in a day and a half, especially on weekends and breaks. She was one of ten students in the room so far. Her teacher, Miss Petty, looked to be in her early twenties, with a pleasant smile and a perfectly rounded afro. *She must sleep with a bowl on her head*, Mavis thought. Miss Petty sat at her desk, surrounded by neatly stacked novels and papers. Mavis took her seat in the center-front of the class.

"Do you mind if I sit here?" a voice asked from her left. She recognized it instantly.

"Sure, go right ahead. I can only sit in one seat at a time," she replied with a smile.

"I'm Elf—remember me from orientation lunch? And I know you're Mavis. Headmistress Menard gave us the full introduction earlier."

"I prefer to be called Madison," she said, finally looking up from her syllabus.

"Okay. So, we're first-years together," he said, tapping his pen on his navy-blue folder.

"Yup."

Princess Francis entered and took the seat on Mavis' other side.

"Okay, class, take your seats," Miss Petty instructed, standing near the whiteboard. The room filled quickly—twenty-five students in total.

She wrote the semester's reading list on the board, then sat to take attendance.

Mavis held her breath. She should've spoken to Miss Petty beforehand about her name.

"Edward Loftus Farrington," she called.

He raised his hand.

"I thought your name was Elf," Mavis murmured, eyes still forward.

"It is. Short for Edward Loftus Farrington," he whispered back.

She smiled. "Right. Elf does make sense."

"Princess Francis," Miss Petty called.

Princess raised her hand proudly.

The roll call continued with students happily claiming their names.

"Mavis Evelyn Madison, Jr."

Mavis wanted to crawl under her desk. She quickly raised her hand and dropped it just as fast.

"Junior?" Elf asked, grinning.

"It's a long story," she mumbled.

"I can't wait to hear it," he said with a smirk.

"Are you always this nosy?" she asked, annoyed.

"I call it inquisitive," he replied, lifting his chin and smiling.

"Eww," she grunted.

Class couldn't end soon enough. She knew Elf was itching to hear more about her name. She packed her bag quickly, then hesitated. Instead of leaving, she walked to Miss Petty's desk.

"Excuse me, Miss Petty," she said, gripping her backpack straps.

"Can you call me Madison, please?" Mavis asked. "Mavis is my mum's name—I'm a junior."

Miss Petty smiled. Mavis held her breath.

Miss Petty's smile softened. "Thank you for telling me, Madison. And I do like the name Mavis—it's beautiful. But I'll call you Madison from now on."

"Thank you so much," Mavis said with a sigh of relief.

"Have a great day, Madison—and happy reading," Miss Petty said.

Outside the classroom, Elf was leaning against the wall.

"So, Junior," Elf said, grinning. "I've gotten ten minutes before my next class. Explain yourself."

Mavis stopped short. "You actually waited outside just to be nosy?"

He shrugged, unashamed. "Pretty much."

"You clearly have too much free time," she said, walking again.

Elf caught up easily. "I have plenty to do," he said. "But yes—tell me how you ended up a junior."

"First of all, don't call me Junior," she said. "Second, it's simple—I'm named after my mother. That's it."

Elf laughed. "I figured. I just wanted to hear you say it." He dodged when she glared. "And for the record—Mavis could've been your dad's name too. It's unisex."

She rolled her eyes. "Thanks. Super helpful." She gave him a light shove.

"You're a violent one, aren't you?" he said, shoving back playfully. "This is my stop." He slowed at the chemistry-room door and held it open.

Mavis gave him a look. "You're enjoying this."

He leaned closer, eyes bright. "Wait—this is your next class too?"

"Unfortunately," she said, drawing the word out.

"Well then—after you," he said, stepping aside with a little bow.

"Just go in," she muttered, nudging him with her shoulder as she passed. He stumbled a step, caught himself at the center desk, and grinned like he'd planned it.

"Elf, I saw that," Axton called from the back, laughing. Elf shot him a thumbs-up and slid into the seat beside Mavis.

"Do you have to sit right here?" she whispered. "Go sit with your friend in the back."

"I like the front," he whispered back. "I actually love chemistry, and I don't want to miss anything." He set out his notebook and pen. He smiled. "Keep rolling your eyes like that and one day they'll get stuck."

"Good," she whispered. "Then I won't have to look at you."

He blinked, a little wounded. "Am I really that bad? You can't be nice to me for one class?"

She exhaled hard. "I don't know you, Elf. You just... inserted yourself into my life and haven't let me breathe since lunch." She waved a hand like she was shooing a fly.

"Geez—okay," he said, holding up his hands. "I didn't mean to be a bother. I just... like you. And you seem like someone I could actually be friends with here."

Guilt pricked her. He was annoying, yes—but he wasn't cruel. And she was being sharp for no reason. She watched him flip through his notes, jaw set like he was pretending not to care. She leaned over and tapped his shoulder. "I'm sorry," she whispered. "I came in too sharp." She held out her hand. "Truce? And... I'm Madison."

He looked relieved. "Truce," he said, taking her hand. His grip was warm and steady. "And I'm still Elf."

"Friends?" she asked, almost daring him to say no.

He grinned. "Friends. We're stuck together for the next six years, right? Might as well."

His eyes lit up, and for the first time, it made her smile instead of scowl.

"Fine," she said, but the word didn't sound as annoyed as she meant it to.

Chapter 8 – The Hologram

Promptly at 9 a.m., a hologram appeared before them.

"Um… were you expecting this?" Elf whispered, keeping his gaze forward.

"No," she whispered back, doing the same.

Elf swallowed. "Spooky, right?"

"Yip," she murmured.

"Maybe it's some kind of chemistry trick," Elf said, trying to sound hopeful.

She frowned. "I doubt it. That man's face looks like he means business."

The image cleared his throat. "Silence. It's time for class. I should be the only one speaking," he said, looking directly at Mavis and Elf.

They sat at attention. Elf's nerves spiked so suddenly his stomach tightened. *Please let the real teacher show up in person,* he thought. *Maybe the hologram is just a one-time thing.*

"I am Dr. Sphinx York. I have a doctorate in chemistry and physics, and I love teaching. You will have the pleasure of being in my chemistry class this school year, and we're going to make it fun. Chemistry is fun, but it's also serious work—so pay attention, hold tight, and let's get this rollercoaster started." He paced at the front of the room. "Now I will take register, and then we will begin Chapter One of your text. Any questions?"

Cynthia came in late; she'd had to stop by the bursar's office to handle a financial matter. She slipped into the desk behind Mavis. Dr. York went silent until Cynthia was seated and her textbook was on the desk. When she looked up and saw him, her knees nearly gave out. Her bag slid from her shoulder and thudded to the floor. She hurried to sit still.

Axton wanted to ask a question but thought better of it. Maybe tomorrow would answer what everyone was thinking: *Was this a one-time thing? Would Dr. York ever show up in person?* No one was brave enough to ask. Instead, their eyes stayed glued to the front—partly from fear, partly from the sense that he would reprimand them for doing anything else.

Dr. York & the Pocket Watch

Mavis wanted to speak up about her name, but she didn't have the gumption. She decided this would be the only class where she'd tolerate being called "Mavis"—unless there were more classes like this. Everyone was distracted by Dr. York, but no one dared let on. Heads stayed bent to the chapter as he went over the information nearly verbatim. He seemed to know they had questions—especially about why he appeared this way—but to this day, no student had the courage to ask.

Relief flooded the room when he said, "Class is dismissed." It felt like a fire alarm had gone off. Students scurried out, many not bothering to pack their books, clutching notebooks as they ran. Mavis—scared beyond measure—packed her bag the way she always did. Even Elf was gone. Even Cynthia, who never would have left her behind, had disappeared.

She could feel the heat of his attention as she stood. *Why is he watching me?* she wondered. It wasn't as if he had to stay behind—he wasn't physically there. She latched her bag, kept her eyes down, and started toward the door. The walk felt like a mile, even though it was only a few steps.

"Lawd, why me?" she whispered, stopping at the threshold and spinning around. "Yes, Dr. York." Her voice trembled. She cleared her throat.

"Come closer," he insisted, standing in front of his desk. Her knees wanted to buckle, but her feet stayed steady as she walked toward him.

"There is only one other Mavis Evelyn that I know, and she was a Thomas at the time of her enrollment."

"Yes, Sir—my mother."

"I know. I can see her features from your nose up. And you are the sister of my favorite twins—Patricia and Ethelyn Louise."

"Yes, Sir."

"How are your mother and sisters?" he asked, to her amazement, perching on the edge of his desk as if he were there in person.

"They are all doing well," she answered politely. Her palms were sweaty and her throat was dry. *It should be the other way around,* she thought.

"I expect nothing but the best from you, Mavis. How have your first few days on campus been?"

"Good, Sir," she said, keeping her hands clasped in front of her.

"Well, that will be all—unless you have a question for me."

She swallowed. If she didn't ask now, she might never ask at all. "Could you please call me Madison?" she blurted.

He folded his arms and regarded her. "And why would I do that, young lady?"

She tried not to sigh. *Is everyone on the 'Keep Mavis' committee?* "Because I prefer Madison," she said. "It distinguishes me from my mother."

"Your mother is not here," he replied sharply, "so there would be no confusion."

She dragged the toe of her shoe across the polished cherrywood floor. "With respect, Sir—my sisters have their own names. All my classmates do. I want to be called Madison."

He studied her—tiny, no taller than 4'11", standing her ground. She had guts. "If that is what you wish, then so be it," he said at last. "But I must tell you—it is an honour to be named after your mother. She was an exemplary student."

"I know, Sir. Everyone always praises my mother," Mavis said, suddenly tired.

"As they should," he said. "Now run along. I don't want you late for your next class."

She turned to go, then hesitated. She felt a little more comfortable now—just enough to risk one more question. "Sir... will you be coming to class tomorrow?"

"Why wouldn't I?" he asked. "I haven't missed a day of teaching here—except for two classes, three years ago."

"Really?"

"Yes. You sound surprised."

She chose her words carefully. "Well, Sir... you missed today. I mean—you didn't come in person."

He went silent. Mavis did too, instantly regretting it.

"This is how I've been teaching class for the past four years," he said at last.

"You have?" she stammered. "But... why?" Her throat was so dry she struggled to swallow.

He smiled, but it didn't reach his eyes. "It will be a story for another time. Now run along to your next class. I have kept you long enough."

"I have study hall in the library next," she said, then realized she was rambling. "I mean... you already know that."

"I do," he said, smiling—almost to himself. "One day, perhaps you can solve my mystery. Until then, I will see you tomorrow." The hologram flickered, and then he was gone.

Mavis stood where he'd been for a long moment, baffled by the exchange and by his reasons for teaching this way. He could have kept anyone after class, yet he chose her. Surely other students had relatives he'd taught too. She shrugged, slung her bag higher on her shoulder, and walked out—no need to hurry now. She wasn't afraid anymore.

Chapter 9 - Newspapers

Toppy passed Mavis in the hallway and greeted her, but Mavis didn't notice. She was too absorbed in what had just happened. Her mind spun with questions: *What is Dr. York's story? Why is he a hologram?* He'd been deliberately vague, making her wait for the truth. That alone made her itch to uncover it faster. Students bumped her shoulders as she walked, but she barely registered it. Entering the library in a trance, she headed straight to the back section—no windows, no distractions – she wanted to sit alone in her thoughts. After a few minutes, she snapped out of it. An idea struck: *The library keeps old yearbooks.* Her mother had graduated in 1991. Maybe she could find Dr. York's photo. She rose and walked two shelves over. The yearbooks were dusty, their spines faded. She scanned the titles until she found it—*The Glasswinged Butterfly.* She remembered flipping through her mother's copy over the summer, giddy with anticipation for her own adventure. The 1991 edition had a red-and-silver suede cover. She opened it carefully. The first four pages listed faculty and staff. Her fingers raced down the rows of photos in alphabetical order. He was one row up from the bottom.

"Here you are, Dr. York," she whispered. He looked younger, but unmistakably him. She stared at the photo, and for a moment, it felt like he was staring back. The hair on her arms stood up. His skin was a golden-yellow hue, his hair trimmed close to the scalp, a black goatee perfectly manicured. Large silver-framed glasses perched on his nose. He must've been in his forties then. Now, he had to be in his seventies—but his hologram still looked sharp, well-maintained. She read his bio: head coach for the boys' baseball and basketball teams, swim coach for the girls, and co-ed golf coach. Captain of the Red Lettered House—still the reigning champions in house competitions against Silver Lining and Lobster Crow.

Mavis was fascinated. *Why her?* Why had he chosen to speak to her—to linger after class? She couldn't ask her mother; she'd immediately suspect a sleuthing mission. Patricia might be a better option. And if needed, Uncle Adrian could help her dig deeper. There had to be something beneath the surface. No place was this perfect; there was always something hidden in plain daylight. She rubbed her hands together, delighted. "Finally," she whispered, "you're going to be my project, Dr. York."

The bell rang for lunch. She glanced at the clock above the librarian's counter. "Drats—it's already 11:50," she muttered. She wanted more time to research, but Headmistress Menard would love nothing more than to roast her for being late.

Her eyes drifted to the shelves below the yearbooks— newspapers, tightly stacked. She knelt and bent the tops of the headlines to check the years. The first stack was from 1973. "This will take forever," she groaned, rifling through another stack. Finally—2018. She grabbed the first five. She had five minutes to get to the dining hall. She rushed to the librarian's desk, nearly twisting her ankle.

"I haven't seen anyone take interest in these besides faculty," the librarian said, stamping the cards on the left of each paper. "Is this for an assignment?"

"Uh... yes, Ma'am," Mavis lied. She couldn't exactly say she was investigating her chemistry teacher.

"Enjoy," the librarian said, handing them over.
Mavis snatched the papers from the counter and bolted toward the dining hall.

Dr. York & the Pocket Watch

Chapter 10 – The Rebuke

Mavis was winded by the time she reached the buffet line; papers tucked under her left arm and a plate in her right hand—just in the nick of time.

"What's all this?" Kimp asked, standing to her left. "Research," she said quickly, shifting the stack higher in her arms.

"Mavis..." she heard faintly behind her. She turned just in time to see Headmistress Menard striding past, heading to her table.

She exhaled in relief.

Sliding into her seat beside Cynthia, she whispered, "You scurried out of class and left me there with a hologram."

"Girl, he scared the life out of me—and I'm a Christian," Cynthia confessed, pointing at herself.

"What does being Christian have to do with being afraid?" Cynthia blinked. "Okay... that didn't make sense, did it?"

Mavis shook her head. "Nope. Not even a little. But anyway—everyone ran out like the room was on fire."

Cynthia laughed. "Indeed."

Mavis carefully placed the newspapers on top of her backpack under the table, hoping no one would trip or spill anything on them.

"What's with all the newspapers?" Cynthia asked, biting into her chicken salad sandwich.

"More research," Mavis said, taking a sip of her conch chowder.

"Uh-huh. Research for what class?" Cynthia asked, skeptical.

"It's personal," Mavis replied, brushing off the question.

"Yup. I figured. And I want no part of that 'research,'" Cynthia stressed.

Changing the subject, Mavis pointed at her bowl. "This is so good."

Cynthia finished her sandwich and stood to get a slice of lemon meringue pie—just as Menard approached.

"Mavis, I'm sure you have better table manners than this," came the voice from behind.

Mavis' eyes rolled before she could stop them.

"Why are you shoveling food into your mouth like we're mixing cement for plaster?" Menard scolded. Mavis stared at the platform-black shoes first, then forced her eyes up to the tight bun perched atop Menard's head. Menard stood with her arms folded, waiting.

Mavis swallowed. "Sorry. It's so delicious—I couldn't resist," she said, trying to mask her irritation.

"Do your best to contain yourself. This isn't a race to see who finishes first," Menard snapped. Her attention shifted to Blain, the senior table captain. "And you—set the tone at this table. I expect refined behavior, etiquette, and grace."

With that, she turned and exited the dining hall.

Cynthia sat frozen through the rebuke, then finally exhaled. "Okay. Now I can get that pie."

Blain rolled her eyes. "That woman knows exactly how to push my buttons."

"Mine too," Mavis muttered. "She's always on my heels."

Franny sat quietly, chewing slowly. She had no intention of getting involved. Her daddy always said, *"Don't tickle the gator unless you're ready to shoot it."* She wasn't about to stir trouble she couldn't escape.

After lunch, Mavis, Cynthia, and Franny headed off to the second half of their day. Franny had gym, Cynthia had music, and Mavis was headed to art.

Chapter 11 – The Xandria Exchange

"What's with all those books?" Willow asked Toppy as she dragged into the room after her last class. Willow was already seated at her desk, working on assignments.

"Homework and research," Toppy groaned, tossing her books onto the floor and flopping onto her bed.

"You poor dear," Willow said sympathetically. "I've only got two assignments, so I'm free during study hall— to shower and call my friend Tae, she texted me this morning wanting to catch up."

"Lucky you. I think I'm working on my thesis for biology," Toppy moaned, "so much work—and I'm not even in college yet. I'm only in seventh grade," she whined, kicking off her oxfords and flicking her socks off with her big toe.

Willow returned to her homework, reaching for her reading glasses beside the desk lamp. Within two minutes, Toppy was snoring. Willow decided to let her sleep—she'd feel better after a nap.

Xandria, a girl who lived three doors down from Mavis and Cynthia, knocked to return the calculator she'd borrowed for math. Mavis opened the door.

"Is Cynthia here?" Xandria asked.

"Not yet, but she should be back soon. Do you want to come in and wait?"

"No," Xandria replied, giving Mavis a slow head-to-toe look. Mavis raised one eyebrow.

Mavis kept her smile. "All right. Who should I tell her stopped by?"

"Xandria. I'm three doors down," she said, pointing down the hall. She held up the pink-and-yellow calculator. "I'm just returning this. Tell her thanks."

"Sure," Mavis said, taking it. Xandria turned and walked away. Mavis closed the door and set the calculator on Cynthia's desk.

Cynthia strolled in moments later.

"Xandria returned your calculator," Mavis said, pointing to it without looking up.

"Great. I need it for homework," Cynthia said, plopping onto her bed. "I'm so tired, Madison. My fingers have no energy left. Having English last period is torture."

Mavis was deep into her newspaper stacks—nothing so far in the headlines or obituaries. She leaned over to grab the second paper.

"Did you hear me?" Cynthia asked.

"Uh-huh. You're tired and your fingers are weak," Mavis paraphrased.

"Fine. I'm going to shower. You stay buried in your research," Cynthia said, grabbing her change of clothes. After her shower, refreshed and dressed in a t-shirt and shorts, her hair wrapped in a pink cotton towel, Cynthia returned. "You're still reading those old newspapers? No one in the modern world reads newspapers—everything's online."

Mavis ignored her. She was on the last of her five stacks and still hadn't found anything. She'd have to return them and grab another batch during study hall tomorrow.

Cynthia walked over to the window where Mavis was seated. "You're seriously researching something," she said, peeking over her shoulder. "Any luck?"

"Nope," Mavis replied, dropping the last newspaper with a thump. The papers scattered across the floor to the foot of her bed. "Drats!" she shouted, annoyed.

Cynthia helped her stack them. "What exactly are you looking for?" she asked, knowing she'd regret it.

"Do you really want to know?" Mavis asked, smiling mischievously.

"On second thought—nope," Cynthia said, moving to her desk.

"Suit yourself. You're missing out on something juicy," Mavis teased.

"I doubt it," Cynthia replied sarcastically.

"So... are you up for checking out the antique and pawn shop before study hall?" Mavis asked, fingers twinkling with excitement.

Cynthia leaned her head back. She'd completely forgotten about that. "Why do you want to go there? It's banned."

"Just to have a look. Gees!"

"Ask Willow. She's more adventurous. Or Toppy."

"But I wanted to go with you," Mavis whined, batting puppy-dog eyes.

Cynthia pointed. "Nope. Those eyes don't work on me."

"Fine. I'll ask Willow. Don't say I didn't give you first crack at this quest."

"I'm good," Cynthia said, texting on her phone.

Mavis cut her eyes and headed to the bathroom door that connected to Willow's room.

"Hey, Madison," Willow said. Toppy was still asleep.

"Want to go down to the antique and pawn shop before study hall?"

Willow's face lit up. "Seriously?"

"Yup. So, do you?"

"Absolutely. I love antiquing. And luckily I just finished my homework. All yours, free as bird, well until I have to call my friend Tae, but that's later." She rambled.

Mavis pulled her into their room. "See! Willow's in." She pointed at her. "Are you sure you don't want to come?"

She and Willow gave Cynthia the guilt stare.

Cynthia closed her eyes and turned her back. "Nope. I'll be the one cooking up the alibi in case you two miss study hall—or better yet, get caught."

"She's such a pessimist," Mavis said, laughing.

"Yup. And this pessimist is not trying to get expelled," Cynthia said, pointing at herself.

Willow sat on Cynthia's bed. "Come on, Cyn. You won't get expelled. It'll be fun after such a long day."

"Nope. Nope. Nope," Cynthia said, shaking her head. "But you two go. Let me know all about it when you get back."

"Fine. Leave her. She wants to be a stinky-poo-poo," Mavis said.

Willow laughed.

"And that I shall be—a safe stinky-poo-poo," Cynthia replied.

Chapter 12 – The Heist

The sun was setting—just the cover Mavis needed. Willow had gone to change into something "more appropriate," while Cynthia sat with her earbuds in, leafing through her history textbook.

Mavis tapped Cynthia's shoulder. "Are you sure you don't want to come?"

"I'm sure," Cynthia replied, eyes still on her book.

"I'm going to knock for Willow. I'll see you before study hall."

"Please be safe. I like having you as my roommate and friend."

Mavis smiled. "Aw shucks, you really do care. I'll be fine—no worries."

She didn't need to knock. Willow walked through the bathroom door, striking a pose.

"I'm ready," she announced. "Let's see what's been hiding all these years in the antique and pawn shop."

"What are you wearing?" Cynthia asked, frowning and pulling out her earbuds.

"It's my camouflage couture," Willow said in a faux-French accent, spinning for dramatic effect.

Mavis laughed. "You look like we're going on a heist. What's with the all-black get-up? We're just looking around."

"Well, yeah—I don't want anyone to recognize me."

Cynthia laughed. "They'll recognize you faster in all black. You look like a full spread on a security camera."

Mavis nodded, but there was no time for a wardrobe change. "Let's get going," she said, pulling Willow toward the door. "See you, Cyn." As they stepped out, Mavis poked her head back in. "What's that? You want to join us?" she teased.

"You're funny. Nope. I'll be right here. Have fun," Cynthia replied without looking up.

Mavis was nervous. Menard had a reputation for knowing when she was doing something wrong—actually, when she was just breathing. She scanned the area as they exited the dorm and walked swiftly along the cobblestone trail toward the stables. Willow skipped ahead, humming. Other students lingered between dorms or sat on benches. Only Mavis and Willow were heading in the opposite direction. Willow began doing cartwheels.

"Willow," Mavis called, just loud enough to get her attention.

Willow stopped and waited for her to catch up. "What?"

"Stop all your jiving," Mavis said. "We don't want to be seen. Someone's bound to notice us."

"Right. Sorry. Not much farther, right?"

"Nope. Just behind those casuarina trees," Mavis said, pointing.

To her relief, they made it undetected. A large chain and rusted metal lock secured the antique and pawn shop's door.

"Drats, I don't know how to pick locks," Mavis said, disappointed.

"Step aside. I can pick a lock in my sleep," Willow boasted, cracking her knuckles.

"You can?" Mavis asked, impressed.

Willow examined the lock. "Hmm. The usual. Nothing fancy." She unraveled her bun, pulled out a large metal hairpin, and worked it into the lock.

Click. It popped open.

"See. Now we may enter," she said, removing the chain.

Mavis E. Madison, Jr.

Dr. York & the Pocket Watch

"You're the best," Mavis said, impressed.

"I know," Willow replied, blowing on her fingertips.

"I've got my flashlight. Don't turn on any lights," Mavis instructed.

"By the looks of this place, I doubt there are any," Willow joked, bumping into a dusty table. A book fell to the floor. "Oops," she said, picking it up and setting it back. "This place is filthy," she added, covering her nose with her sleeve. "I feel a sinus attack coming on." Still, she touched everything within reach.

Mavis was drawn to a table near a dust-blackened window. "What's this?" she asked, picking up a navy blue leather bound book with a key still in the latch.

Willow coughed. "Are you trying to give us both asthma?"

She took the book and turned it over. "It's a diary."

"Yeah, but why would it be here? Who pawns a diary? Or considers it antique?"

She turned the key and opened it.

Willow wandered off, distracted by a lace shawl draped over a rocking chair. It was too stained for her taste. She returned to Mavis, who was flipping through the diary.

"Anything   interesting?"

"Hmmm," Mavis frowned.

"I'd leave it. It's probably junk. Might have bugs—and they'll end up in our rooms."

"Nah, I already flipped through and shook it out. No bugs. We're safe from ancient infestations."

"If I see one bug in my room, I'm coming for that diary—and burning it," Willow warned.

She looked around some more, but nothing caught her eye. It was getting darker. Mavis turned on her flashlight, keeping the beam low to avoid drawing attention. She touched a pair of glasses, then spotted a pocket watch. It had a plain silver case and a crystal crown atop the winding stem.

"That's neat," Willow said.

"Yeah. I'm keeping this too."

"Hey, we better head out. Study hall's soon."

"Yeah, let's go. Maybe we can come back this weekend."

Willow frowned. "Nothing in here feels antique. Pawn, maybe. But antique? Definitely not." She pulled the chain and lock from her pocket and secured the door as they'd found it.

Mavis checked the coast—clear. "Let's run to the stables, then walk casually from there."

They sprinted to the stables, then strolled along the cobblestones back to their dorm. Mavis couldn't wait to read the diary. The pocket watch was a bonus—she loved timepieces. Her grandfather had been a watchmaker and repairman.

"Where are you two coming from?" Blain asked as they passed her dorm, Davis-Greene.

"Just taking a walk before study hall," Willow said quickly. Mavis nodded in agreement.

"What's that under your arm?" Blain asked, reaching for the diary.

Mavis shifted her body. "Just my book."

"You read and walk?" Blain asked, unconvinced.

Mavis smiled and kept walking. Willow close behind.

"See you at breakfast," Blain called after them.

Chapter 13 – The Garage

"Hustle, girls," Ms. Biggertoe called as Willow and Mavis passed her open door. "You're cutting it close to study hall."

They hurried past, slipping into their rooms just in time.

"I was worried," Cynthia said as soon as Mavis closed the door. "But I knew Biggertoe would have her door open, and I couldn't get to the stairs or elevator."

"Blain stopped us along the way," Mavis replied, placing her new finds on her desk.

"What was it like in there?" Cynthia asked, curious as she opened her math textbook.

"It was old and dusty. Willow mostly complained, and the lighting was terrible. But I found a used diary I can't wait to read—and a pocket watch," Mavis said, settling into her seat by the window.

The sun had already set. The sky was so dark it seemed invisible—no stars, and a moon that barely showed its face. She stared out into the emptiness, thinking about everything that had happened since arriving at Thomas-Scott Academy. Her mind buzzed with thoughts of Dr. York and the secrets that might be tucked inside the diary. She went to the bathroom to wash the dust from her hands, then returned to her desk and opened her chemistry textbook. Dr. York had assigned chapters two and three for tomorrow, plus a take-home quiz. He'd left an impression on her—one that made her feel like she needed to give her absolute best. Not just in chemistry, but in everything. She also had a chapter to read for literature and a short film to watch. Behind her, Cynthia was struggling with math. Scrap papers flew into the small iron mesh trash bin like snowballs. Mavis turned around, distracted by the flurries.

"Cyn, what are you doing?"

"I can't get this stupid problem right. I think the answers at the back of the textbook are just there to torture students."

Mavis walked over and leaned over the book. "Which problem?"

"This one," Cynthia said, pointing with a sigh.

Mavis grabbed a loose-leaf sheet from her binder and started scribbling. "It's so simple—that's why it's stumping you. Sometimes the brain overthinks what's actually easy."

Dr. York & the Pocket Watch

"Simple?" Cynthia groaned. "I've been working on this for thirty minutes."

"You start by moving what's on the left to the right. Watch," Mavis said, walking her through the steps. "Do you understand it now?" she asked.

"You make it seem so easy."

"I love math. I'll help you anytime. You'll ace it—I promise. Do the next one so I can see you've got it," she said, pulling her chair closer.

Cynthia tackled the next problem step by step.

"You got it, Cyn! You got it!" Mavis clapped.

Cynthia hugged her. "You can tutor me. I'll pay you in ironing and plaiting your hair."

"Deal," Mavis said, shaking her hand. They laughed and returned to their homework's.

An hour later, "I'm so hungry, Madison. How much longer?"

"I'm done—just reading this diary."

"Anything interesting?"

"Hmmm... I need to brush up on my Madlemorian."

"Your what?" Cynthia asked.

"Madlemorian. The language they spoke here until 1901."

"I thought they always spoke English."

"Nope. They spoke both. The aristocrats kept using Madlemorian beyond 1901 to separate themselves."

"Interesting. But I'm hungry. Can you brush up on it later?"

Mavis laughed. "Sure. I'm hungry too."

"Let's get food from The Garage. I heard it's opening tonight."

Mavis had heard about the great food at The Garage—the eatery on the first floor of their dorm. Each dorm had one, but with a different name.

She saved her page with a napkin bookmark.

"Hey, where are you two going?" Toppy asked, stepping out of her room.

"We're going to The Garage for some grub-a-dub-dub," Mavis replied.

Toppy laughed. "Me too. Willow wants me to bring her something—she's about to shower."

Cynthia pressed the elevator button. Biggertoe's door was still ajar.

"Goodnight, Ms. B," they said in unison.

"Night, girls," she replied, her room the scent of moth balls and lavender; her eyes glued to her nightly soap opera.

The line at The Garage stretched outside the entryway. Cynthia's stomach rumbled louder.

"That drum is a rum-pa-pum-pumming," Toppy teased.

"I'm starving," Cynthia said, hugging her stomach.

The line moved quickly.

"Darlin,' what'll it be?" asked a slender woman behind the counter.

"Meatball stromboli with salt and pepper fries, please," Cynthia said.

In less than two minutes, she had her foil-wrapped stromboli and fries in hand.

"And you, darlin'?" the woman asked Mavis.

"Peanut butter and banana sandwich with pickle fries and apple juice, please."

"What kind of order is that?" Cynthia asked.

"I like it. You should try the pickle fries."

"I'm good. I'll pass," she said, laughing.

"Here you go, darlin'," the woman said, handing over the food.

They waited for Toppy outside. By the time she came out, Mavis and Cynthia were nearly done with their fries.

"Madison, that was a pregnant woman's kind of order," Toppy teased.

They all laughed.

"Willow told me you went to the antique and pawn shop," Toppy said once they were safely behind the elevator doors.

"Yup. She wasn't impressed, though."

"Yeah, she said that. But she enjoyed going with you."

"Next time, you should join us," Mavis said.

"Of course. Let me know."

"Cyn, want to come?" Mavis asked.

"Still a no for me."

"Come on, Cynthia—we're the four musketeers," Toppy said.

"There were only three. You all have your quorum," she replied.

"Fine. Keep being a stinker," Mavis pouted.

Chapter 14 – The Diary

Cynthia turned on the TV, volume low of course—Mavis had returned to reading the diary. Cynthia finished her stromboli with a loud burp, followed by a giggle. "Excuse me," she said, covering her mouth.

Mavis looked over, shook her head, and returned to the diary.

Cynthia, bored with the TV, joined Mavis on her bed, sitting on the opposite side. "Anything good?" she asked. "You can't seem to put it down." She leaned closer, furrowing her brows. "What are you reading?"

"Huh?" Mavis asked, puzzled.

"There's nothing on the page," Cynthia said, pointing at the yellowed paper.

"Of course there is," Mavis replied, tracing her finger across the words.

"Madison, I don't know what you're seeing, but those two pages are blank."

"Cyn, stop playing around. It's in Madlemorian. See—I'll read this line." She pointed. *"'I should have listened to mother, but it's too late now.'"*

Cynthia stared at her. "I'm telling you; those pages are blank. I'll get Willow or Toppy. They'll prove I'm not crazy—and that you're seeing things."

She knocked on the bathroom door.

"Hey, Cyn. Come in," Toppy called, still eating her conch salad.

"Come—I want to show you something. Tell me what you see," Cynthia said, leading her back to the room.

"That's a cool diary, Madison," Toppy said, sitting beside her.

"Toppy, tell her what you see on that page."

Toppy looked. "Nothing. Will you be using it yourself?" she asked Mavis.

"See. I told you."

"You don't see anything, Toppy?" Mavis asked, confused.

"Nope. It's blank. Did Willow look at it with you?"

"No. She wanted me to leave it behind—thought it might be infested."

"Willow," Toppy called.

She came over.

"What do you see?" Toppy asked, pointing to the page.

"That old junk! I told Madison to leave that bug hotel in the pawn shop," Willow said, wrinkling her nose.

"But what do you see?" Toppy asked again.

Willow looked at them, confused. "It's an empty diary. What's the big deal?"

"It's not empty," Mavis insisted. "It's Maeve Brynn's diary—and it's written in Madlemorian."

"Who's Maeve Brynn? And what's Madlemorian?" Toppy asked.

Mavis sighed, rolling her eyes and closing the diary. "Didn't any of you know they spoke Madlemorian here until 1901?"

"No," Toppy and Willow said in unison.

"Well, they did. And this girl's diary is in that language. Maybe she was an aristocrat—or just wanted privacy."

"If it is a dead language that only the aristocrats speak, how do you know it?" Cyn asked, the others sat looking at Mavis curious.

"My mother speaks it, she was born here and she made it a point to learn it. She taught my sisters and I; my dad was not interested in learning it."

"Oh." Cyn remarked, and the others nodded their heads.

Willow getting up to leave, "Madison, you've had a long day. Get some rest. That diary's empty and old. Maybe you inhaled a bug and it's messing with your brain," She said, eyeing the diary with suspicion.

"Fine. Don't believe me. It's mine now, and I'll read it and enjoy it," Mavis said, placing it on her desk.

"See you later. I've got more reading to do," Toppy said, heading out. Willow followed.

"Madison, we weren't making fun of you," Cynthia said gently. "But really—that diary is blank. I hope it's not haunted and you're seeing something the rest of us can't."

"It's not haunted."

"Anyway, I'm going to shower and get to bed. We've got Dr. York first thing. I hope he shows up in person."

"Yeah. I'll shower after you."

"I was supposed to plait your hair. Want me to do it before I shower?"

"Sure, but will it hurt?" Mavis asked, frowning.

"No," Cyn replied. "Bring me your comb, brush, and hair grease."

"I don't use hair grease," Mavis replied.

"So you don't moisturize your scalp?" Cyn asked, incredulous.

"No. I wash it with raw aloe extract, moringa oil, and coconut oil shampoo and conditioner. Sometimes I deep-condition with just the aloe," Mavis said.

"Okay. I'll use some of mine," Cyn said. "Get your comb and brush and come sit." She pointed to the floor by her chair.

"May I watch the TV while you butcher my hair?" Mavis asked.

"If you must," Cyn replied.

Mavis sat on the floor between Cynthia's knees and handed her the comb and brush. Then she turned on the TV to a comedy show. Cyn started at the roots and worked her way down to the tips. Mavis screwed up her face in agony, jerking her head back and forth in protest.

Cyn tapped her lightly on the crown. "Keep still, or it'll hurt more."

"I thought you said it wouldn't hurt," Mavis grumbled.

"If you'd detangled it properly, it wouldn't," Cyn said, not missing a beat. "But now I've got extra work. Before I can plait it, I have to detangle it."

Mavis groaned. "I think my scalp will need stitches after you're done. It feels like ants are gnawing at my head." Mavis continued, "but I'm sure I'll need a hair transplant. Every time you rake that comb across my head like a lawnmower, I swear my hair is falling out."

Cynthia couldn't help but laugh. "All done detangling. I gained muscles for sure." She flexed one arm. "Now I'm going to section it and grease it before I plait it."

"I don't think I can take any more. Can we just leave it detangled?" Mavis whined.

"No, because it'll get tangled up again," Cyn said, parting it. "No pain, right?"

"No—because my head has gone numb," Mavis said, still whining.

"Oh, my Lawd. Such a big baby," Cyn said. She greased Mavis's scalp, parted her hair into two sections, and cornrowed each side, securing the ends with small clear rubber bands. Then she curled the ends around the tip of her rat-tail comb. "All done—and you survived."

"Barely," Mavis moaned.

"Go take a look. It looks lovely," Cyn said.

Mavis got up and went to the full-length mirror, running her hands over her hair. Despite herself, she smiled.

Cyn leaned back in her chair. "Was it worth the pain?"

"I love it, Cyn. I will need painkillers when my scalp wakes up, but thank you—I absolutely love it," Mavis said, grinning.

"It won't be painful next time, because I cleared it out," Cyn said.

"Next time?" Mavis clutched her head. "I'm keeping this until we graduate. I'm not letting you mow across my scalp again."

Cyn laughed. "I'll do it again in three days. You'll get used to it. And if we have time, I can do smaller plaits—those can last about a month, maybe longer."

Mavis shook her head. "I don't think I can take smaller. Two is fine for now."

"Okay—until your next hair appointment," Cyn said. "Tie it down at night, okay?" She grabbed her clothes and headed to the bathroom.

Mavis really loved her hair; it was the first time it had ever been styled like this. She couldn't stop glancing at herself in the mirror.

Then she went back to the diary. She wasn't haunted or crazy—she knew what she saw. She couldn't resist reading more. *"Miriam and I should have left things just as we saw them, but curiosity got the best of us. Now everyone is scurrying to return things as they were. If only I had listened to Mother. Oh, Mother—why did I not listen?"* She looked out the large window at the dimly lit courtyard. The wind was high tonight, leaves rustling like foil. She wondered why her mother and sisters had never mentioned the antique and pawn shop. Maybe they'd listened. Maybe they'd never gone inside.

"All yours," Cynthia announced, stepping out in pink and orange pajamas.

Mavis was still at the window, staring into the courtyard. Cynthia joined her.

"It's so dark tonight," she said.

"Hmm. Yeah, it is."

"Are you okay?" she asked, concerned.

"I'm good. Just wondering what's the big deal about the antique and pawn shop. It seemed... ordinary."

"Stop thinking about that place. What matters is that it's restricted. I hope you're not planning to go back."

"Yeah, yeah, yeah. I heard you."

"I was worried about you and Willow. I wish you hadn't taken anything. What if someone checks inventory? Madison, please—leave that place alone."

"I heard you."

"But are you listening? It's not worth it. Menard's on you like flies on fresh fish. Leave well enough alone."

"I'm going to shower. Stop worrying. Menard doesn't scare me. She annoys me—but she doesn't scare me."

Cynthia stayed at the window, watching the darkness. Mavis went into the shower. Curiosity got the best of her. Cynthia picked up the diary, flipping through the pages carefully, not losing Mavis' marked spot.

Nothing. Absolutely nothing.

She considered praying over the book—but what if it was haunted? She didn't want that spirit following her. She quickly closed it and doused her hands in sanitizer, waiting to wash them properly when Mavis came out.

Chapter 15 – Silence had Consequences

Elf and Axton were already seated at the front of the class when Mavis and Cynthia entered. Seats weren't assigned, so students could sit wherever they liked. Cynthia preferred the middle. Mavis took the same seat she had yesterday. Class was filling up. Elf and Axton were deep in conversation—this was the first time Elf hadn't instantly acknowledged her, and to Mavis' relief, she enjoyed the quiet. She pulled out her textbook, a binder of loose-leaf paper, and her iPad and pen, ready for class to begin. Turning slightly, she saw Cynthia three seats behind her in the same row. They exchanged smiles and crossed their fingers before Mavis turned back around.

At 9 a.m., Dr. York appeared—just like yesterday, but in a different suit. He began taking attendance and announced that labs would start next week once supplies arrived. The room went still. As he paced, he glanced at Mavis. A few students noticed the attention and started watching her instead. Their eyes made her shift in her seat. She tried to focus, but his movements kept pulling her gaze back. Then she spotted it: a pocket watch dangling from his left pants pocket. It was identical to the one she'd found in the antique shop. *Coincidence—or not?* Her stomach tightened, tugging her toward the belief that the two were connected. Dr. York stopped pacing. She realized she'd been staring. She snapped her eyes to her page just as his gaze met hers.

"Madison, stay focused on your pages," he scolded.

"Yes, Dr. York," she said, cheeks burning.

"Any questions?" he asked, scanning the room. Silence.

"Don't be shy. I won't bite," he added. Still, no one spoke. "Okay, since we have no questions—books away. Take out a loose-leaf paper. We're having a quiz."

Low murmurs rippled through the room. No one had expected this.

"Silence," he bellowed, his voice echoing like an empty barrel rolling downhill. A few students jumped in their seats. "You had your chance to speak. Now let's get on with the pop quiz," he said sternly.

He fired off question after question about the periodic table. Pens raced across paper. He wanted to teach them a lesson: *silence had consequences.* This would help him decide who to call on next time.

"Okay, pass your paper to the person beside or behind you. You'll correct each other's work."

Cynthia hated peer correction—it was always awkward. Mavis didn't mind. She handed her paper to the girl behind her.

"My name's Madison," she said.

"I'm Zoe."

"Good luck," Mavis said. Zoe smiled and wished her the same.

"Return the papers to their owners. All who got five or fewer wrong—raise your hands."

Mavis proudly raised hers. So did Zoe and Cynthia.

"Those with more than five wrong—brush up on your periodic table. We'll have pop quizzes regularly. The reason I did this today is to encourage you to ask questions. I'm here to help you understand chemistry. Get over how I look—I'm still your teacher. Understood?"

"Yes, Sir," they chorused.

The bell rang. Mavis wasn't the last to leave this time. She didn't want another scolding about distractions. She practically ran out. Dr. York noticed but didn't stop her.

"Hey, Junior—wait up!"

She groaned. Only Elf called her that. How many times had she told him to use 'Madison'? She kept walking.

He caught up. She was headed to the library for study hall—eager to return her first five stacks of papers and grab more.

"Hey, Madison."

"Elf."

"I got a low score on that quiz. Thought I knew the material."

"Did you rush?"

"We all did. He breezed through those questions like it was a racetrack."

"He did go on a bit of a rampage, didn't he?"

Elf chuckled. "Yeah. Why do you have all these newspapers?" he asked as they reached the library.

"I'm reading them," she said, shifting the stack in her arms.

He blinked. "People still read newspapers?"

"Not really," she admitted. "But my dad and I used to read them every Saturday." She nodded toward the doors. "You have study hall too?"

"I do," he said. "I'm going over my answers… and sulking a little."

"It's the first quiz, and he isn't grading it," Mavis said. "Don't be so hard on yourself."

The librarian arrived. She raised her eyebrows as Mavis set the bundle down. "Back already?"

"I'm a fast reader," Mavis said. "I'd like to check out more."

"All right," the librarian said. "I'll log these back in. Come find me when you're ready for the next batch. I'll be right here," she added with a small smile.

Elf followed her toward the tables. "Mind if I sit with you?"

"Sure," she said. "As long as you're not about to cry over your quiz."

"I won't," he said, smiling.

He dropped his bag beside hers and grabbed a golfing magazine from a nearby aisle. He tilted his head at her new stack. "More from 2018?"

"I'm looking for something specific," she said, scanning the headlines.

Elf lowered his voice and leaned closer. "Madison… why are you really reading these?" His expression softened. "You can trust me."

She sighed. "I'm curious about Dr. York. About what happened to him."

"Why do you think the papers will help?"

"Maybe they wrote something about him."

"You think something bad happened?"

She folded the paper. "Yeah. Don't you? It's strange that he teaches as a hologram. I'm curious who's creating the images. Maybe it's him—but why?"

"Want my help?"

She blinked, surprised. "You'd do that?"

"Of course," he said. "I want to know what happened to him too."

"I saw his photo in the 1991 yearbook—my mum's graduating year. I wondered if the papers mentioned him. So, I'm reading all of 2018."

"He's been like this that long?"
"Yeah. He told me when I asked after class."

"Wow. We all wanted to know—but were too afraid to ask."

"Grab a stack from 2018," she said. "We can read during study hall. And I won't ask you to take any home unless you want to."

"I don't mind. I'm quick with homework. Plus, you've got me curious now. Is anyone else helping?"

"No. I've been working solo."

"Okay—just us then." He extended his hand.

She shook it. They'd come a long way since their first meeting.

They grabbed more stacks—three for her and five for him. Mavis watched Elf start at the top of the first page, reading every line.

She nudged him. "Elf—you don't have to read every word. Just skim for 'York,' 'Sphinx,' or anything about the science department."

He grinned sheepishly. "Okay, okay."

"Did you know this school was built on a cemetery? It was the only affordable property."

"No," he said, mouth agape. "Where'd you hear that? That would be really creepy."

"My mum, I think. Are you afraid of the dead, Elf?"

"No, not at all. I always ask my mother to come to me in a dream."

She looked at him with sudden seriousness. "Your mother is dead?" she whispered.

"Yip," he said. "That's why I'm here. My dad remarried, and next thing I knew, I was registered—and now I'm here."

"Oh my God that is so sad."

"It is?"

She touched his hand. "I'm sorry, Elf. I'm so sorry."

"Thank you," he said solemnly. He missed his mother more than he liked to admit.

"So, do you have brothers and sisters?" she asked.

"Nope. Not yet—but soon, I guess," he said with a small shrug.

"Wow. I feel so sorry for you," she said. "Why did you choose to be my friend from day one?"

He shrugged. "I just liked you—that was it. No reason at all." She'd half expected him to say she reminded him of his mother. When he didn't, she felt oddly disappointed.

"Well, we're friends—and my father always wanted a son. I'm sure I can convince him to adopt you. You're my brother now," she declared.

He smiled. "I have a father, Madison."

"I know," she said quickly. "But you're my family now. My dad can be your second dad. And my mum—she can never replace your mum, but I'm willing to share her with you."

A warm smile spread across his face, and his eyes went glassy. He wiped them quickly. His dad always scolded him when he cried—said men didn't cry, that they controlled their emotions. "Thank you, Madison," he said softly. "I appreciate you. You're the first person here to know my mother has passed. I don't want too many others to know. I don't want pity—I want genuine friendships."

She leaned into his shoulder. "It'll be just between us— siblings' secret. Well... my parents and my sisters will have to know because you're family now." Then she straightened. "Now let's get back to work."

He saluted, smiling. "Yes, ma'am."

"Shhh," she hissed, and they both giggled.

Elf leaned back in his chair, still holding the newspaper, his eyes scanning the tiny print as if it might reveal more. "I wonder if anyone else knows about this," he said softly. "I mean, if he really went missing... and now he's teaching us like nothing happened."

Mavis nodded, her mind racing. "It's like he vanished but never left. That's what's so strange. If he's alive, where is he? And if he's not...?"

"Then who's behind the hologram?" Elf finished her thought.

They sat in silence for a moment, the weight of the mystery pressing between them. The hum of the library faded into the background, replaced by the sound of their shared curiosity.

"I think we need to go to the antique and pawn shop," Mavis said, her voice low but firm. "There's more there. I can feel it."

Elf looked at her, uncertain. "You really think we'll find answers in that dusty place?"

"I don't know," she admitted. "But I found the diary there. And the pocket watch. It's like breadcrumbs."

"Okay," he said, nodding slowly. "I'm in. But we need to be careful. If Menard finds out...."

"She won't," Mavis said, her eyes gleaming. "We'll be ghosts."

Elf chuckled. "You're the ghost. I'm the guy who trips over his own feet."

She smiled. "Then I'll be your lookout."

They gathered their papers, stacking them neatly on the table. Mavis tucked the article into her notebook, marking it with a sticky tab. Elf stood and stretched, his shoulders still heavy with emotion.

"Thanks for listening," he said quietly. "About my mum. I don't talk about her much."

"You don't have to thank me," Mavis replied. "You're my friend. My brother, remember?"

He smiled again, a little softer this time. "Yeah. I like that."

They walked toward the exit, the library's warm light casting long shadows behind them.

"Six-thirty," Mavis said as they reached the door. "Meet me by the stables."

"I'll be there," Elf said. Then he hesitated. "And Madison?" She looked back. "What?"

"Let's just be careful," he said.

"For sure." She was headed to P.E. next. Swimming was the unit for the next four weeks, then soccer after that. She loved watching soccer, but she wasn't the best at playing it. As Mavis stepped onto the pool deck, the scent of chlorine hit her nose like a familiar memory. Aquamarine tiles shimmered under the overhead lights, and the water looked like liquid glass. She loved this part of the day—where her body could move freely and her thoughts could drift toward solving mysteries or decoding the diary. She dove in cleanly, slicing through the water with practiced ease. For a few minutes, she was just Mavis—the girl who swam like a dolphin, who felt most herself when submerged. But even underwater, her mind tugged at the breadcrumbs of the puzzle: the diary, the pocket watch, and the newspaper clippings.

When she surfaced, Franny was already lounging at the edge, kicking her feet.

"You swim like you're trying to escape something," she teased.

"Maybe I am," Mavis replied, wringing water from her hair. She showered, washing the stench of chlorine from her curls— she already knew Cynthia would insist on doing it again tonight because it looked frizzy. She dressed quickly, still thinking about everything that had happened so far. She felt optimistic that she and Elf would uncover the truth. It was good to have someone else on the quest to solve the mystery of Dr. York and his pocket watch.

Chapter 16 – Cyn's Stress

"Cyn, you need to wear a tam on your head and sweat out that cold," Mavis told her when she walked into the room. "Sit in the steam from the shower, then bundle up. And put on your socks too."

Cynthia groaned. "I hate sweating out my colds."

"Yes, I do too," Mavis said, "but it works. It never fails. My grandmother made us sweat out our colds. We felt worse that night, but better the next day." She headed toward the diary on her desk.

Cynthia rolled her eyes. "You and your imaginary diary," she said, then coughed.

"See. You've got a cough now. You need to wrap up, Cyn." Mavis opened her trunk. "I've got cerasee tea in here. I'll fix it with lemon—I grabbed some from the dining hall because I had a feeling you'd need it. And did you take that Covid test I left on the desk?"

Cynthia sighed. "Yes. It was negative. So it's just a cold—thank God."

"Yeah—thank God," Mavis said. "I would hate to be stuck in quarantine. Come on, let's get you some cerasee and lemon."

Cynthia watched as Mavis dug out a box of tea. "That trunk of yours is like a mishmash of a grocery store and a pharmacy," Cyn said, trying to laugh, but her headache wouldn't let her.

"I'm going to the antique and pawn shop tonight with Elf," Mavis added, "but I'll get you straight before I go."

Cynthia's eyes narrowed. "Madison..."

Mavis held up her hands. "I know—the Garden of Eden."

"Make jokes—I'm serious," Cynthia said between coughs. "Menard has it out for you, and you keep tugging at the bait. Play with it long enough and she'll catch you."

But Cynthia could've saved her breath. Mavis was already fixing the cerasee, stirring in lemon after squeezing it into the hot tea.

"Here—drink this and inhale the steam," Mavis said, handing her a small green cup with an orange frog handle. "I'll mix you some honey and lemon too."

Cynthia took a careful sip, then winced. "Madison, I will worry. I don't like you going down there."

Mavis waved a hand. "I won't be alone. Elf is going with me, and Willow is coming to pick the lock."

"Lawd... you have Willow picking locks," Cynthia said, holding her head.

Mavis paused, eyeing her. "You're acting like she's committing a crime."

Cynthia screwed up her face as she swallowed another bitter sip. "Well, isn't she? I think it's called breaking and entering."

"She offered, and I accepted," Mavis said. "We'll be careful, Cyn."

Cynthia held up a hand. "I don't want to know anything else. Just go—and get back safely."

Mavis grinned. "Thank you, Mother, for your permission."

Cynthia sucked her teeth. "There's no use telling you not to—you'll go anyway. I'm sick, and you're stressing me out. And look at you, hair still wet. Are you trying to get sick too?"

Mavis rolled her eyes. "I'll turn on the shower for you and get your warm clothes ready. I'll wrap you up before I go."

Cynthia groaned. "Madison, I'm serious—you're stressing me out."

"Well, next time come with us and see that it's harmless," Mavis said.

Cynthia shook her head. "Nope. Not me."

"Take your tam into the bathroom," Mavis instructed, handing her the lime-green tam.

Mavis rummaged in her trunk until she finally found the camphor rub—buried beneath packs of oatmeal. Cynthia went into the shower. When she came out, she was dressed warm from head to toe, robe included. She was already burning up, but she knew Mavis would insist and persist.

"I found the camphor rub," Mavis said. "Let me put some under your nose and on your feet. You can rub a little on your chest too."

Cynthia moaned, already sweating. "Do you think all of this is necessary?"

"Yes. You'll thank me in the morning," Mavis said. "You're lucky I don't have an onion to put under your feet." She tugged off Cynthia's cotton-white socks, rubbed the bottoms of her feet with the camphor ointment, then slid the socks back on.

Cynthia sat and watched, too tired to argue. "Now lie down," Mavis added. "Rub your chest while I put some under your nose." Cynthia complied.

Cynthia frowned. "What are you doing now?"

"Wrapping you up further," Mavis said, pulling the quilted pink-and-brown floral blanket up to Cynthia's chin. "I'm leaving this honey-and-lemon mix for you to sip in intervals while I'm gone. Try to sleep too—I won't be long."

Cynthia arched an eyebrow. "Yes, Dr. M... any further instructions?" she asked dryly.

Mavis brightened. "I like that—Dr. M. I might just become a doctor. Something to think about."

Cynthia's voice softened. "Madison, please be safe."

"I will," Mavis promised. "And you start sipping that mix. Before you can finish it, I'll be back—okay?"

Cynthia sat up in bed, the blanket still tucked beneath her chin and began sipping the honey-and-lemon mix.

"Good patient," Mavis said, then slipped out.

Mavis closed the door behind her. The hallway was dim and quiet; most students were still at dinner or winding down. She headed toward the stables; her damp hair tucked under a hoodie. The diary was zipped inside her backpack along with the stamped newspaper. Elf was already waiting by the fence, hands in his pockets. He looked up as she approached.

"You made it," he said.

"Of course," Mavis said. "I'm not backing out now."

"Willow's already there," he said. "She texted me—said the lock's being stubborn."

"Stubborn?" Mavis asked, raising an eyebrow.

Elf gave a small shrug. "She said she has tricks."

They set off together, footsteps soft on the gravel. Casuarina branches swayed overhead, whispering in the wind. Mavis felt that familiar tug in her chest—equal parts thrill and dread. When they reached the shop, Willow was crouched at the door, her flashlight wedged between her knees, hairpin buried in the lock.

"About time," Willow muttered without looking up. "This thing is ancient."

Elf tried to lighten the mood. "Maybe it's meant to stay locked."

"Not tonight," Willow said. With a final twist, the lock gave way. She stood and brushed off her knees. "There."

Mavis eased the door open. Dust and stale air rolled out. She clicked on her flashlight, the beam cutting a pale path through the dark. They stepped inside. Mavis went straight to the corner table where she'd found the diary. Elf drifted to the shelves of books and trinkets. Willow hovered near the door, arms crossed, keeping watch.

"Anything with a name," Mavis whispered. "Maeve Brynn. Miriam. Dr. York."

Elf nodded, already flipping through a stack of faded pamphlets.

Willow lifted a cracked photo frame and squinted at the sepia-toned picture. "This place is giving me the creeps," she muttered.

Mavis ignored her and focused on a small wooden box tucked beneath the table. She slid it out and wiped away a layer of grit. A brass clasp held it shut—no lock. Inside were folded papers, brittle with age. She opened one and froze. It was a letter, written in Madlemorian. Her pulse jumped. "I found something," she breathed.

Elf and Willow hurried over.

"What is it?" Elf asked.

"A letter," Mavis said. "Same language as the diary. It's signed... M.B."

Willow's eyes flicked to the signature. "Maeve Brynn?"

"Could be," Mavis answered. "I'll translate it later. But this— this matters."

For a beat, none of them spoke. Even Willow's sarcasm vanished. The wind worried the casuarina branches outside, and the shop seemed to hold its breath around them.

Willow exhaled sharply. "Okay. We got what we came for. Let's get out of here before Menard shows up with a flashlight and a fury."

Mavis slid the letter into her backpack. Her hands were unsteady. "Let's go," she whispered. "We've got reading to do."

By the time Mavis slipped back into the dorm, the wind had picked up and the air felt sharper. She eased the door closed behind her and crossed the room on quiet feet. Cynthia was curled under the quilt, still asleep, the honey-lemon mix half-finished on the nightstand. Mavis set her backpack on the desk and carefully unfolded the letter. The paper was brittle and the ink faded, but the Madlemorian script was clear enough to work with. She opened her notebook to the back—where her translation notes were growing—and began.

"To those who find this: beware the temptation to uncover what was meant to remain buried. Miriam and I were warned. We did not listen. Now the balance is broken, and the echoes of our choices linger in the halls we once walked."

Mavis paused, her pen hovering. The phrasing was strange—poetic, almost. She read the next line aloud, softly.

"The watch was never meant to be worn again. It marks more than time—it marks the moment everything changed."

Her breath caught. The watch. Dr. York's watch.

She flipped back to her notes from the diary. Maeve Brynn had mentioned Miriam. She'd written about regret, about not listening to her mother. And now this letter—warning of consequences, of something broken.

She looked over at Cynthia, still asleep. The camphor rub glistened faintly under her nose.

Her phone buzzed. A message from Elf.

"Have you read the letter yet?"

"I have, and it's both intriguing and scary," she replied.

"Let's talk tomorrow. Sleep tight, Junior."

She smiled despite herself. He was growing on her—the brother she'd always wanted. And "Junior" no longer offended her.

She tucked the letter into her notebook and turned off the desk lamp. But sleep wouldn't come. The words kept looping through her mind: *"The watch was never meant to be worn again."* And yet... it hung from Dr. York's pocket like a warning.

She wasn't sure when she drifted off, but it felt like she'd only just closed her eyes before it was time to get up for class. She was anxious to see Elf and Willow—there was so much to discuss. The auditorium was half-lit, the bamboo ceiling fans spinning lazily overhead as students trickled in. Mavis, Elf, and Willow sat close together in the far-left corner beneath the antique portrait of Mrs. Wilhelmina Thomas-Scott, their heads bowed and voices low. Cynthia wouldn't be joining them today; she was feeling a bit better, but the nurse had given her the day off to rest. Mavis had left her in bed with honey-lemon tea, a tam pulled snug over her braids, and a cup of chicken noodle soup warming in the hotpot. She planned to sneak up during lunch to check on her.

"I translated more of the letter last night," Mavis whispered, pulling out her notebook. "It's definitely Maeve Brynn. And she keeps mentioning someone named Miriam."

Elf leaned in. "What did it say?"

Willow, still skeptical but intrigued, crossed her arms. "Let's hear it."

Mavis flipped to the page, her finger tracing the lines. "She wrote: *'Miriam and I were warned. We did not listen. Now the balance is broken, and the echoes of our choices linger in the halls we once walked.'*"

Willow raised an eyebrow. "Sounds like they messed with something they shouldn't have."

"Exactly," Mavis said. "And then there's this: *'The watch was never meant to be worn again. It marks more than time—it marks the moment everything changed.'*"

Elf's eyes widened. "The watch. Dr. York's watch."

Mavis nodded. "I think it belonged to Maeve. Or maybe Miriam. Either way, it's connected."

Willow leaned forward. "So, who's Miriam? A friend? A sister?"

"I don't know yet," Mavis said. "But I think they were close. Maybe even roommates like us. There's a line in the diary that says: *'Miriam said we should leave it buried. But I couldn't. I had to know.'*"

Elf rubbed his chin. "Leave what buried?"

"That's what we need to find out," Mavis said. "I think it's something they found—maybe in the shop. Or somewhere on campus."

Willow glanced around the auditorium. "You think it's still here?"

"I think whatever it was... it started something. And now we're caught in the ripple."

The bell rang faintly in the distance, signaling the start of assembly. Students began filing in, voices rising, chairs scraping. But the three of them stayed huddled, their circle tight.

"We need to find out who Miriam was," Elf said. "If she was a student, she'll be in the yearbooks."

"We can check the yearbooks after assembly," Mavis said.

Willow stood, brushing off her skirt. "I still think this is all spooky. But I'm in. Just don't ask me to read any ghost letters."

Mavis smiled. "Deal."

They joined the rest of the students, slipping into their seats as Father Trent stepped onto the stage. But their minds weren't on the prayer or the announcements. They were on Miriam. On Maeve. On the watch that marked more than time. And on the secrets still buried beneath Thomas-Scott Academy. The morning assembly passed in a blur. Mavis barely registered Father Trent's prayer or Deputy Headmaster Ying's announcements. Her mind was already in the library, flipping through yearbooks in search of Miriam. As soon as they were dismissed, she, Elf, and Willow slipped out ahead of the crowd, ducking into the library's back entrance, thankful for the thirty minutes break before their first class. The librarian gave them a nod, already familiar with Mavis' routine.

"Yearbooks are two shelves over," Mavis whispered, leading them to the archive section.

Willow pulled out the 2019 edition, its spine cracked and faded. Elf grabbed 2020. Mavis went straight for 2018—the year her sisters graduated.

They sat at the long wooden table beneath the stained-glass window, the morning light casting fractured colors across their pages.

"Start with the faculty and staff," Mavis instructed. "Then check the student index. Look for Miriam Brynn. Or just Miriam."

Elf flipped carefully, scanning each name. "No Miriam Brynn in 2020. But there's a Miriam E. Langston. She's listed as a Red Lettered House captain."

"Same house as Dr. York," Mavis noted.

Willow leaned over. "She's in 2019 too. Same person, same name. She must've been a senior in 2020."

Mavis opened the 2018 yearbook. Her sisters' photos smiled back at her from the student council page. She flipped to the alumni notes—there was a mention:

"Miriam Langston, Class of 2020, awarded early honours in chemistry and co-authored the Red Lettered House Science Journal with Sphinx York."

Her heart skipped.

"She worked with him," she whispered. "They were close."

Elf leaned in. "So, Maeve and Miriam were probably students here together. And Dr. York knew them both."

Willow frowned. "This is getting deep. What if they found something? Something dangerous?"

Mavis nodded slowly. "The diary said they were warned. The letter said they broke the balance. And now... Dr. York teaches as a hologram."

Elf flipped to the faculty page. "He's listed in 2020 as Head of Science. But there's no photo. Just a note: *'On sabbatical.'*"

Willow raised an eyebrow. "Sabbatical or something else?"

Mavis closed the book gently. "We need to find the Red House Science Journal. If they co-authored it, maybe it holds answers."

The librarian passed by, shelving a stack of returned books.

"Excuse me," Mavis said. "Do you have archived copies of the Red Lettered House Science Journal?"

The librarian paused. "That's a rare request. But yes—we keep them in the restricted archive. You'll need permission."

"From whom?"

"Headmistress Menard." She replied.

Willow groaned. "Of course."

The librarian returning to her desk.

Mavis looked at them both. "We'll find another way."

They gathered their books, minds buzzing. Outside, the courtyard was quiet, the wind still whispering through the casuarina trees.

"Miriam Langston," Mavis said softly. "She's the key." Then it hit her, she gripped both of their hands, "didn't Dean French mention that the antique and pawn shop has been closed for fifty years?"

"Yeah." Elf replied, "and…?"

"Well, isn't it strange that the diary and the watch were recently put in there—sometime between 2018 and 2020?"

Silence.

"That is strange." Willow agreed.

"Do you think Dean French has something to do with this as well?" Elf whispered.

"There's a cover-up," Mavis said. "If she isn't fully involved, then she at least knows something. And who knows who else? The whole administration—including Menard—might be in on it."

Willow shivered. "We're in deep quicksand. I just hope one of us is holding the magic rope to pull the rest of us out."

"No need to be afraid," Mavis said. "My Uncle Adrian is a private investigator. If this gets too intense for us, I'll call him, and he can solve the mystery on our behalf. So… are we still all in?"

"I'm still in," Elf said.

Mavis looked at Willow, who still looked uneasy. "And you?"

Willow gave a small, worried laugh. "I have to be in. Who else is going to pick the locks?"

Mavis smiled. "Exactly."

Chapter 17 – Time is not merely a Measure

The library was quieter than usual. Cynthia was still tucked away in their dorm, wrapped in camphor and quilts, sipping honey-lemon tea, and texting Mavis updates between naps. Mavis, Elf, and Willow had returned to the archive section, determined to find the Red Lettered House Science Journal. But the journals were locked behind a glass case, and the librarian had been clear: no access without Headmistress Menard's written permission.

Willow's eyes flicked to the lock. "I vote we pick it."

Elf glanced around. "And I vote we don't get expelled in our first month."

"Then we need someone who knows the system," Mavis whispered. "Someone who's been here long enough to know the shortcuts—and the loopholes."

Willow tapped the desk with her left pointer. "Then we don't ask for the journal. We ask for something harmless that gets us close to it."

Mavis nodded slowly. "We need leverage—an assignment, or a teacher who'll request it without asking too many questions." Her gaze flicked toward the desk. "And we need it to look like it was their idea. Miss Petty," Mavis decided. "She's kind, and she won't report us just for asking a question. I'll talk to her after literature." She turned to Elf. "Find out who the Red Lettered House captain is this year—and if they're connected to the journal." Then she looked at Willow. "And you—figure out when the librarian takes breaks. If we need one quick minute at that case, timing matters. Meet back here at lunch," Mavis added. "Same table, same whisper level."

They nodded and spread out, careful to look like three students doing ordinary work — separating with practiced calm—books closed, faces neutral. But Mavis could feel the glass case behind them like a magnet.

Elf's mind was racing; there must be a way to get access to the journals without needing Menard's approval — he knows they would never get it. Meanwhile, Willow was thinking if they came into the library at night she could get a quick crack at the lock, they can take photos of the pages they needed and return the journal as if it were never touched. But then sense kicked her in the midst of her thought, her mind asked her if she was nuts. *Are you preparing for a life in juvie hall or you just don't want a future?* Her mind scolded.

They were anxious walking in together at lunch. Mavis knows that Blain for sure would notice that she is not at the table, but this was important she just had to solve this everything within her says it has to be done. Just as they took their seats, as if he had been listening from behind the walls to them earlier a voice is heard before he is seen.

"So you guys are interested in the Red Lettered House Science Journal?"

Willow's palms began sweating, "how did he know and better yet, is he faculty? Are they in trouble?"

Careful. "Why?" A curious Mavis inquired.

"Oh I heard you asking the librarian earlier. She is no help really."

"And you are?" She asked, cautiously.

"I could be."

"Um, we are good." Willow chimed in, she did not have a good feeling about him.

"Are you sure?" He asked smugly. "I know you do not want to ask Menard for permission; I may have a way to help you."

"And why would you be willing to help us?" Elf inquired.

"So you do want access to the journal?"

Willow looked across at Elf, he felt uneasy like he had exposed a secret.

"Listen, I've read every issue," he said, adjusting his glasses. "Twice."

Mavis curios. "Do you know how to access them?"

Gideon smirked. "Technically, no. But practically? Yes."

Willow raised an eyebrow. "What's the difference?"

"Rules are for those who don't know the loopholes," he replied. "Follow me."

He led them to a side door near the librarian's office. "This used to be the facility archive. They moved most of it, but the journals were too fragile to relocate. There's a vent behind the poetry shelf that leads to the old filing room."

"A vent?" Elf asked, skeptical.

"It's wide enough. I've used it before. I was researching Dr. York's early experiments. He was supposed to mentor me, you know. But then Miriam Langston came along."

Mavis caught the bitterness in his voice. "You knew her?"

"Not personally. But I knew of her. Everyone did. She was brilliant. York chose her for the Red House Science Journal. I submitted three proposals. He never responded."

Willow leaned in. "So, you've been holding a grudge?"

Gideon shrugged. "I prefer to call it… unfinished business."

"Are you a teacher here?" Elf asked curiously.

"I am a former student here. At present, I am at the university studying biomedical science and sometimes I come by to use the lab for personal research." He replied.

"Oh." They chorused.

He pulled back the poetry shelf, revealing a narrow metal vent. "It's dusty, but it'll get you there. I'll keep watch."

Mavis looked at Elf and Willow. "We're really doing this?"

Elf grinned. "We've come this far."

Willow cracked her knuckles. "Let's go."

They crawled through the vent, emerging into a dim room lined with filing cabinets and old wooden shelves. The journals were stacked neatly in a corner, bound in red leather with gold lettering.

Mavis pulled out the 2020 edition. Inside, she found an article co-authored by *Miriam Langston and Sphinx York* titled *"Temporal Displacement and the Ethics of Scientific Memory."* She read aloud: *"Time is not merely a measure—it is a vessel. What we place in it echoes beyond our understanding. Our experiment proved that memory can be preserved, but at what cost?"*

Elf looked stunned. "They were experimenting with memory?"

Willow frowned. "What does that even mean?"

Mavis flipped to the back. There was a photo—Miriam and Dr. York, standing beside a strange machine. And behind them, barely visible, was the same pocket watch.

She traced the image with her finger. "They did something. Something that changed him."

Elf whispered, "And maybe… changed everything."

They sat in the old filing room, surrounded by dust and silence. Willow had wedged the vent open for air, while Elf flipped through the journal's appendix.

"There's a diagram," he said, turning the book toward Mavis. "It looks like... a machine. Wires, coils, something like a transmitter."

Willow squinted. "That's not chemistry. That's physics. Maybe even quantum."

Mavis read the caption aloud: "*Prototype for memory preservation and projection. Designed to store cognitive patterns and simulate presence.*"

Elf leaned back. "You think that's what Dr. York is using now?"

Willow crossed her arms. "You're saying he's not just a hologram—he's a projection of stored memory?"

Mavis nodded slowly. "It's possible. If they built this... and something went wrong..."

Elf flipped to the final page. "There's a note. Handwritten. Not part of the article."

He read aloud: "We were warned. *The machine works—but not without cost. York is changing. He forgets things he should remember. Remembers things that never happened. I fear we've fractured something we cannot repair.*"

Willow's face paled. "That's not just spooky. That's dangerous."

Mavis closed the journal, her hands trembling. "We need to find the machine."

Elf looked at her. "You think it's still here?"

"If York is still teaching—still appearing—then something is powering it. And if it's affecting him..."

Willow stood. "Then it could affect others."

They crawled back through the vent, Gideon waiting with his arms crossed.

"Well?" he asked.

Mavis handed him the journal. "You were right. Miriam and York built something. Something that shouldn't exist."

Gideon's eyes gleamed. "I knew it. I knew she wasn't perfect."

Elf stepped forward. "She wasn't the villain, Gideon. She tried to stop it."

Observant. "You seem surprised." Willow remarked, "I thought you read the journals, and more than once." Looking skeptically at him.

Stammering, "I have…but I did not read this one. I guess it was checked out at the time." He replied.

"Interesting." She said, not convince.

Dismissively, "it does not matter. What matters is that York and Miriam were working on something that was unethical."

"It doesn't matter now, it is history." Elf said.

"To you maybe, but for me it is vindication, because I always knew she was a goody-goody and that she and York were going against the wishes of the administration."

"You are such a bitter little man." Willow remarked, "so bitter."

"If it weren't for this bitter, little man you would not have access to this. And by the way, why do you even care about this journal?"

"Just doing research, scientific research." Elf quickly answered.

Gideon shrugged. "Well. I want credit when your research is a success, I contributed." He insisted.

Willow rolled her eyes. "You'll get a footnote."

They slipped out of the library, the morning sun casting long shadows across the courtyard. Mavis felt the weight of the journal in her backpack—and the weight of what they'd just learned.

Dr. York wasn't just a teacher. He was a memory. A projection. A warning.

And somewhere on campus, the machine still hummed.

Chapter 18 – The Red House Rebels

Chemistry class was unusually quiet. Cynthia was back, bundled in a soft gray hoodie, her braids tucked under a tam, and her voice still raspy from the cold. Mavis gave her a warm smile as she slid into the seat beside her. Elf took his usual spot near the front, Willow beside him, flipping through her notes with a practiced flick. Mavis on the other side of Elf, her notebook already open to a fresh page. The trio exchanged subtle glances—there was a rhythm to their collaboration now, a silent understanding.

Kimp, Pierson, Toppy, and Axton noticed.

"Since when are they a trio?" Kimp whispered to Toppy, nudging her elbow.

"Something's up," Axton added, leaning forward. "They've been whispering in the library, skipping lunch, and now they're synced like a jazz trio."

Franny, seated two rows over, raised an eyebrow. "I say we find out what they're up to. I hate being left out of a good mystery."

Dr. York appeared at exactly 9:00 a.m., his hologram flickering slightly before stabilizing. He wore a navy-blue suit today, the same pocket watch dangling from his left pants pocket. "Good morning, scholars," he said, voice smooth and commanding. "Let's begin."

As he paced the room, Mavis watched him closely. He remembered her name, her mother's graduation year, even her sisters' names. But Miriam's warning echoed in her mind: *"He forgets things he should remember. Remembers things that never happened."* So why did he remember her family so clearly? She scribbled a note in the margin of her notebook: *What if the machine stores selective memory? What if it's being updated?*

Dr. York paused mid-lecture, eyes locking with hers. "Madison, would you care to explain the difference between ionic and covalent bonding?"

She stood, heart thudding. "Ionic bonding involves the transfer of electrons between atoms, typically between a metal and a non-metal. Covalent bonding involves the sharing of electrons between two non-metals."

"Excellent," he said, nodding. "Your mother would be proud."

A few heads turned. Cynthia blinked. Kimp mouthed, *See.*

After class, Mavis, Elf, and Willow were gathering their things when Kimp approached.

"Okay, spill. What's going on?"

Toppy and Axton flanked her. Franny leaned against the doorframe; arms crossed. Pierson waited patiently for an answer, leaning against the wall near the doorframe.

"You three are up to something," Axton said. "And we want in."

Willow raised an eyebrow. "You want in on what, exactly?"

"Whatever this is," Franny said. "The glances, the library dives, the secret notes. You're chasing something—and I hate being left out."

Mavis looked at Elf, then Willow. "Meet us at The Garage after study hall. We'll talk."

Later That Night – The Garage

The Garage was buzzing. The basement dining area was alive with chatter, the scent of strombolis and pickle fries hanging in the air. Mavis, Elf, Willow, Cynthia, Pierson, Kimp, Toppy, Axton, and Franny squeezed into a corner booth, snacks piled high.

Cynthia sipped her tea, still wrapped in a blanket. "The cold must have distorted my brain – I wanted no part of this and now here I am. Please someone check my forehead." She griped. Deep down she had been worn down, her curiosity now gets the better of her and Mavis was relentless.

Mavis pulled out her notebook, flipping to the translated letter. "We found a journal. Co-authored by Miriam Langston and Dr. York. They built a machine—one that stores memory and projects presence."

"Wait, like... holograms?" Axton asked.

"Exactly," Elf said. "But it's more than that. It's like York is... preserved. But not perfectly."

"He remembers my family," Mavis said. "But Miriam wrote that he was forgetting things. Remembering things that never happened."

Franny leaned in. "So, what if someone's updating the machine? Feeding it selective memories?"

Willow nodded. "Or protecting certain truths. Madison made note that Dean French wanted us to stay clear of the antique and pawn shop, stating that it was closed for fifty years, but the diary and the pocket watch states differently they were placed there more recent like between 2018-2020."

"The antique and pawn shop, you have been there?" Franny asked, surprised.

"Ah yes," Elf replied.

"But it is forbidden." Axton remarked.

"I told them." Said Cyn, "but these three have insisted on testing Menard's desire to expel Madison."

"So what is it like in there?" Kimp asked intrigued.

"Dusty, dirty, and dark." Said Willow.

"Sounds like a place I want no part of." Said Franny.

"I would love to go." Said Kimp."

"Okay, we are getting off topic." Said Mavis, "yes we went to the antique and pawn, we found a diary written in Madlemorian." And before they could ask, "she explained the language hoping for the last time. "And we also found the very pocket watch that Dr. York wears daily."

"That is scary." Franny remarked diving her long pink spoon into her root beer float.

"So now what?" Axton asked, "what exactly are you three trying to do?"

"Isn't it obvious?" Asked Willow.

"No." Said Kimp.

Rolling her eyes, "we are working together to solve the mystery of why our chemistry teacher is a hologram and the significance of the watch he is wearing."

"Ah, oh!' Said Kimp. "But how?" He asked confused.

Willow was exhausted by him, too many questions.

"We need to find the machine he and Miriam created, it is somewhere on campus and maybe we will get answers there."

Axton, "count me in, you have me interested. I am curious about him."

"Me too." Added Franny. "Sounds interesting and exciting."

Kimp grabbed a fry. "This is wild. So, what's next?"

"We find the machine," Mavis said. "And we figure out what it's really doing."

Toppy raised her soda. "To the Red House Rebels."

They clinked cups, fries, and foil-wrapped sandwiches. The mystery had grown—and so had the team.

Chapter 19 – The Glitch

Chemistry class began like any other. Dr. York materialized at precisely 9:00 a.m., his hologram flickering once, then stabilizing. He wore a charcoal suit today, the silver pocket watch gleaming against his vest. His voice was steady, his posture impeccable.

But something was off.

"Today we'll be discussing the properties of noble gases," he began. "Argon, neon, krypton, and—"

He paused.

"—and… and…"

His image stuttered. The watch glitched, spinning unnaturally. His voice distorted, like a scratched record.

"—and… Miriam, no—no, not now—"

The class froze.

Cynthia sat upright; eyes wide. Elf leaned forward. Mavis' heart pounded.

Dr. York's projection shimmered, then snapped back into place.

"Excuse me," he said, voice calm again. "Let's continue."

But the damage was done.

After class, the group gathered in the courtyard behind the science wing. Mavis, Pierson, Elf, Willow, Cynthia, Kimp, Toppy, Axton, and Franny huddled beneath the casuarina trees, their voices low.

"He said Miriam," Mavis whispered. "He glitched. He remembered something—or someone."

"And not just remembered," Elf added. "It was like he was… reliving it."

Willow crossed her arms. "We need to find the machine. Now."

Franny nodded. "We split up. Cover more ground."

They divided into teams:

- **Team Archive**: Mavis and Elf would return to the library to search for blueprints, schematics, or any mention of the machine in faculty records.
- **Team Red House**: Willow, Toppy, and Axton would investigate the Red Lettered House dormitory—

rumored to have hidden compartments and old storage rooms.
- **Team Admin**: Cynthia, Kimp, Pierson, and Franny would scan the administrative wing, looking for keys, access codes, or forgotten files.

They agreed to meet at The Garage at 7:00 p.m. to share findings.

Team Archive – Library

Mavis and Elf combed through dusty faculty binders and old science journals. In a folder labeled *Experimental Technologies – 2018*, they found it: a blueprint.
It was labeled *Cognitive Projection Unit – CPX-1*. The diagram matched the machine in the yearbook photo. Notes in the margins read: *"Memory tether unstable. Risk of temporal bleed."*

Elf looked at Mavis. "Temporal bleed?"

"Like... memory leaking into the present. Or the past bleeding into now.

Team Red House – Dormitory

Axton led the way, flashlight in hand. In the basement of Red Lettered House, behind a false wall in the laundry room, they found a locked cabinet. Willow picked the lock with a bobby pin. Inside: a journal. Not Maeve's—but Miriam's.

Toppy lifted it carefully. "This is old. Really old. Like it was a used diary that she found and wrote in the blank pages."

Willow flipped through the pages, frowning. "It's written in that same weird script. Madlemorian, right?"

"Yup," Axton confirmed. "Definitely not English."

Willow closed the journal gently. "We'll take it to Madison. She's the only one who can read this."

Toppy nodded. "Let's not mess with it. If it's anything like Maeve's diary, it could be sensitive."

Willow tucked it into her satchel. "Preserved and protected. Madison will know what to do."

Team Admin – Office Wing

Cynthia, Pierson, Kimp, and Franny snuck into the old admin records room. In a drawer labeled *Faculty Incidents*, they found a report: *Dr. Sphinx York – 2019 – Sabbatical Request Denied.*

Franny read the note: "*Subject refused to cease experimentation. Warning issued. We are monitoring the situation.*"

Kimp whispered, "He never left. He just... changed."

That Night – The Garage

They reconvened over strombolis and soda, the table cluttered with papers, journals, and blueprints.

"He's not just a hologram," Mavis said. "He's tethered to something. Something unstable."

"And it's glitching," Elf added. "He's remembering things he shouldn't. Or things he buried."

Willow laid out Miriam's journal. Mavis read the section she pointed to, "She tried to stop him. But she couldn't."

Franny leaned in. "So, what do we do?"

Mavis looked around the table. "We find the machine. We shut it down. Or we find out what it's trying to tell us."

The room fell silent.

Outside, the wind howled.

Inside, the truth waited.

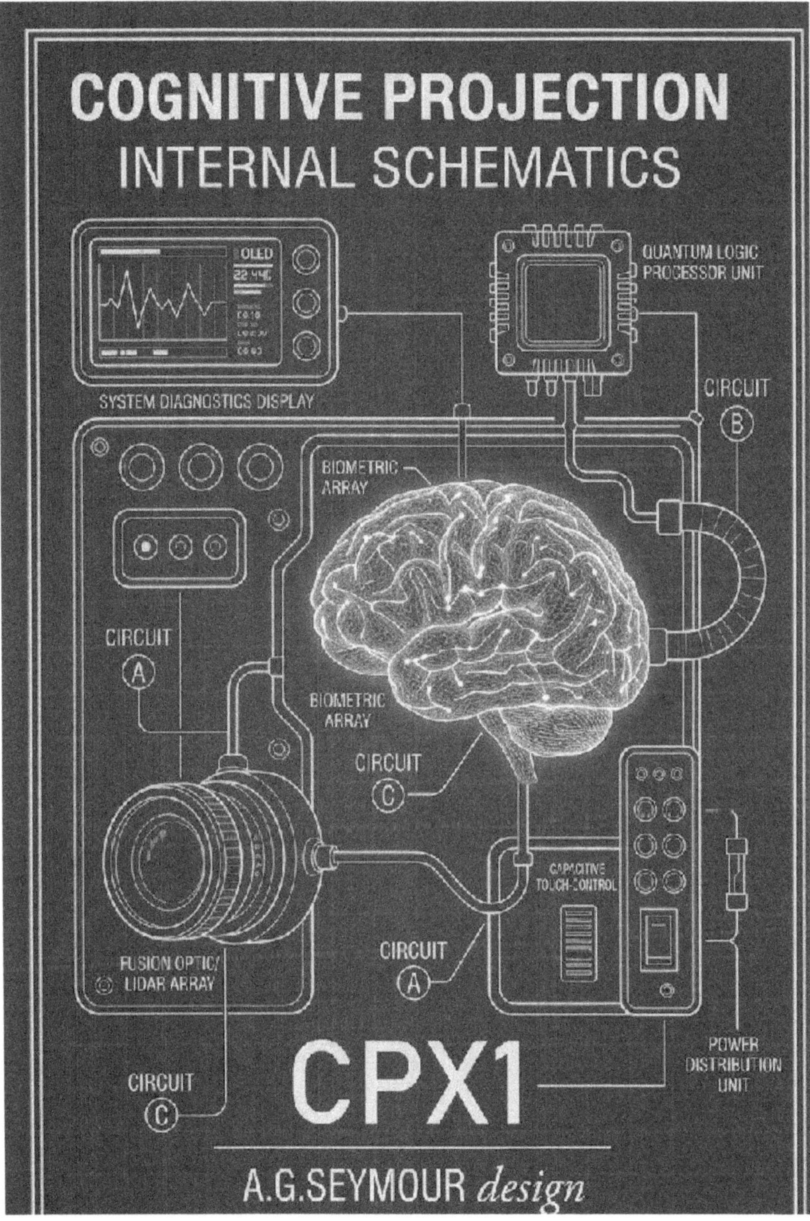
COGNITIVE PROJECTION
INTERNAL SCHEMATICS
OLED
QUANTUM LOGIC
PROCESSOR UNIT
SYSTEM DIAGNOSTICS DISPLAY
CIRCUIT
B
BIOMETRIC
ARRAY
CIRCUIT
A
BIOMETRIC
ARRAY
CIRCUIT
C
CAPACITIVE
TOUCH-CONTROL
FUSION OPTIC/
LIDAR ARRAY
CIRCUIT
A
POWER
DISTRIBUTION
UNIT
CIRCUIT
C
CPX1
A.G.SEYMOUR design

Chapter 20 – Beneath the Furnace

The science wing was quiet after hours, its tiled floors gleaming under the flickering hallway lights. Mavis walked with purpose, Miriam's journal tucked under her arm, her translation notebook ready. Elf and Willow flanked her, their expressions serious. The rest of the crew was scattered across campus, each following a lead. Tomorrow is the start of mid-term break, so they needed to cover as much ground as possible. Elf was going home with Mavis, her parents were excited to have him – his dad was fine with it, he has heard a lot about Mavis, plus he's out the country with his wife on a business trip, it made the burden of finding a sitter for Elf easier. Elf was relieved, he did not want to go home. Cynthia was elated to have a break she missed her family. She had offered for Mavis to join her, but she declined because she had Elf and didn't want him to have to go home to a house sitter and silence. Everyone else would be going home as well.

They had agreed to reconvene at midnight in the old greenhouse behind the biology lab—neutral ground, rarely used, and far from Menard's patrol routes.

Mavis' Translation – Miriam's Journal

Back in her dorm, Mavis sat at her desk, the journal open beside her. The Madlemorian script was elegant, looping, and dense. She translated line by line, her pen moving quickly.

"York believes the machine will preserve him. But it's not preservation—it's distortion. He forgets the present. Remembers the past as if it's now. And sometimes… he speaks to people who aren't there. I tried to shut it down. He refused. Said the academy needed him. Said the students would forget him if he left. I fear he's becoming the machine. Not just tethered to it—but absorbed by it."

Mavis paused, heart racing. *Absorbed?* What did that mean?

She flipped to the final page.

"If anyone finds this, know that the machine is beneath the old Red House lab. Behind the furnace. It hums when no one's listening."

The Search Begins – Midnight in the Greenhouse

The group gathered under the moonlight; their breath visible in the cool night air. Mavis shared the translation. The room fell silent.

"He's becoming the machine?" Axton asked. "Like… he's not just projected—he's trapped?"

"Or worse," Franny said. "He's fading. And the machine is all that's left."

"We need to see it," Elf said. "Tonight."

They split again:

- **Mavis, Elf, and Willow**: Headed to the old Red House lab to find the furnace.
- **Cynthia, Kimp, Pierson, Toppy, Axton, and Franny**: Stayed behind to monitor the courtyard and keep watch for Menard.

Beneath the Furnace

The lab was dusty, abandoned, and smelled faintly of rust and old chemicals. Mavis found the furnace easily—it was massive, cast iron, and cold to the touch.

Willow spotted the panel first. "Here. It's loose."

Elf pried it open. Behind it: a narrow passage, lined with wires and humming faintly.

They crawled through, emerging into a small room. In the center stood the machine—tall, skeletal, and pulsing with a soft blue light. The pocket watch was embedded in its core.

Mavis stepped closer. "It's still running."

Willow pointed to a console. "There's a message."

Elf wiped the dust from the screen. A line of text appeared:

"Welcome, Miriam. Memory sync in progress."

Mavis' breath caught. "It thinks I'm her."

The machine buzzed louder. The watch spun. And then—

Dr. York's voice echoed through the room.

"Miriam… you came back."

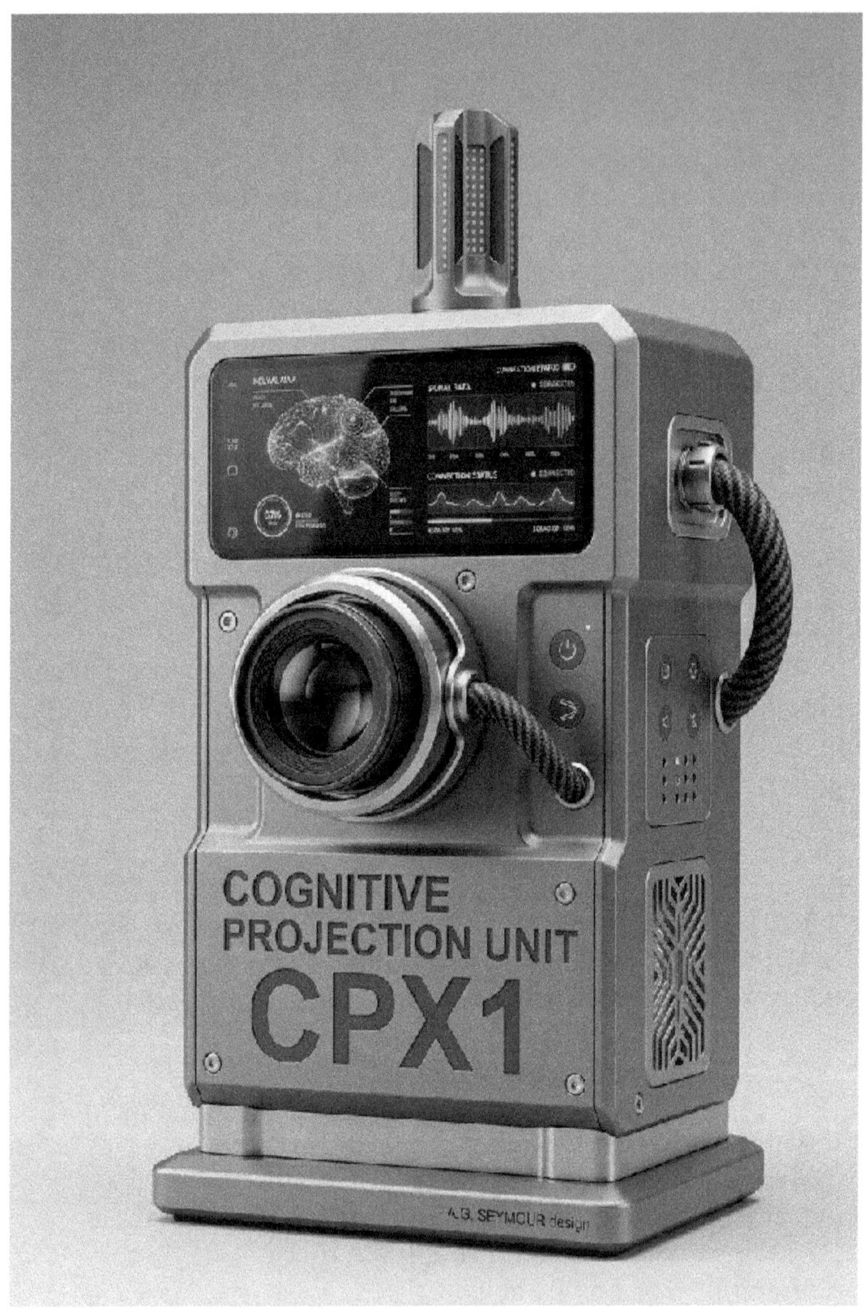
COGNITIVE
PROJECTION UNIT
CPX1
A.G. SEYMOUR design

Chapter 21 – Midterm Break

Unfinished business lingered, but time hadn't been on their side last night. They'd made progress—just not enough. At dawn, cloaked in fog, Mavis and Elf stood ready for the school shuttle to take them to the airport. Cyn had left the night before, happy to be home. Her cough had faded to a whisper, and she felt much better. The others were departing at various times throughout the day. Mid-term break offered a reprieve from the rigors of school, yet they were torn—longing to be huddled together again, unraveling the mystery of Dr. York and his pocket watch.

At the airport, Mavis panicked. Had she left the diary on her desk? Room checks were scheduled during the holiday, and Ms. Biggertoe, along with the other housemothers and housefathers, would be thorough. Elf helped her search. It was tucked inside her cerulean, blue sweater—her favorite. Relief washed over her as she remembered packing it last night after flipping through its pages before bed.

Hand pressed to her chest, she exhaled. "Thank the Lord. I would've been cooked if Biggertoe found this. We can't trust anyone. They could all be in on whatever this is."

"I agree," Elf said. "Are you sure your parents are okay with me coming?" He asked for the third time since they'd left school.

"Positive, Elf. My dad already has plans for you. My mum couldn't be happier—she's always looking for strays to board."

"So, I'm a stray?" he said, mock-offended.

"No, silly. I'm teasing. She loves taking care of people. You're family to us. Even my sisters think of you that way."

His jaw dropped. "Really? Your sisters too?"

"Yup. So, get ready to be overfed and loved."

Grateful, but tinged with melancholy, he murmured, "My dad seemed relieved. Like I'm a burden. Maybe I've always been one."

She touched his shoulder gently. "Don't think that. I'm sure he loves you. Maybe you remind him of your mother, and it hurts. Maybe he's still grieving in his own way."

"I don't know, Junior. He's always been distant. It was always me and my mum. He made excuses to work late. Only when she got sick did he show interest. After she passed, he went back to his old ways. I got the honour of being raised by a nanny or Uncle Fred and his dog, until I came here to Thomas-Scott Academy."

"Elf, that's the saddest story I've ever heard."

"It's my story. And yeah, it's sad."

"Well, chin up and back straight. You're part of the Madison family now. You're loved and always welcome. I told you—my parents would adopt you if you wanted."

"I don't think my dad would allow it."

"Well, if you ever decide, let me know. They're calling our flight."

They grabbed their bags and Elf's box of donuts, then joined the boarding line for their five-hour flight to Coco Plum Cay. Elf loved flying. So did Mavis. They had the middle and window seats—Elf by the window, Mavis leaning over him now and then to catch the view. The gentleman beside them fell asleep moments after sitting down, earphones in, snoring softly. The stewardess, friendly and amused, let them have his share of snacks.

"Best flight ever, right?" Elf said, chewing a croissant filled with strawberry jelly.

"Yup. Two hours left. We can pick another movie or nap."

"No sleeping. Let's find another movie."

They didn't know when they drifted off, but the gentleman gently tapped Mavis' shoulder. "We're here. Wake up your brother."

She smiled and thanked him, seeing no need to correct him. Elf was her brother.

"Elf," she said, shaking his arm. "We landed."

He rubbed his eyes, stretched, and looked out the window. Snow dusted the runway and the distant mountains. Excitement bubbled—snowboarding at the indoor facility, and the downtown all-you-can-eat buffet awaited.

Her mum stood waiting, beaming. Her dad was still at the office but planned to come home early. She hugged them both, kissing their cheeks. "My babies are home."

Elf was stunned. They truly saw him as family—as a son.

Dr. York & the Pocket Watch

In the car, she glanced at him in the rearview mirror. "Now Elf, make yourself right at home. You're not a stranger."

He grinned. "Yes ma'am."

"Good. Tonight, we're heading to your uncle's, Madison. He's got a new dog, and we promised to visit once you two got home."

"Aww, another dog? Is it another Cane Corso?"

"Yes, he loves that breed. Elf, are you allergic to dogs?"

"No ma'am."

"Perfect. My brother-in-law loves dogs, and so does Madison. Just wanted to make sure you aren't allergic."

"I am not. And thank you for having me. My dad says thank you too."

"Think nothing of it. You're always welcome. I'm sorry about your mum. I can't replace her, but I'll love you as if I birthed you myself."

Tears welled in his eyes. "Thank you, Mrs. Madison."

"No, no. I'm Mums M to you now. And my husband is Papa M. We decided last night."

Mavis looked back at him. "See. I told you—they love having you. You're family now."

"Thank you."

"Anything you need, just ask."

They turned up the steep driveway. The house perched on a hill—quaint and elegant, like a winter cottage from a Christmas movie. Inside, it smelled of vanilla and cinnamon. Warm. Inviting.

"Elf, your room's down the hall near the first bathroom. Your name's on the door."

He was thrilled. His very own room. He dropped his bags near the foot of the bed. A basket of goodies sat atop the comforter, along with a caddy of bath essentials. She'd thought of everything. A bookcase filled with adventure novels stood beside a 65" television. The remote rested neatly on the nightstand, next to an antique stained-glass lamp.

Mavis popped her head in, holding her bags. "Do you like your room?"

"I love it."

"Great. I'm just across the hall. Mum's fixing lunch, then we're hitting the streets. Dad should be home by four, but we might still be out."

"Should I shower first, or am I dressed okay?"

She shrugged. "Up to you."

"Are all these books yours?" he asked, pointing to the shelf.

"Nope. They're my dad's. He's had them since he was a boy. Used to read them to me and my sisters at bedtime."

"Wow. I thought they were yours."

"Technically, they belong to all of us. They're part of the house. I'll unpack and see you in twenty for lunch."

"Sounds military," he joked.

She laughed. "Just be ready."

"Yes ma'am," he said, saluting.

"Dad, this is Elf," Mavis said, gesturing to the boy standing shyly behind her. "Don't be shy, Elf. Dad, tell him not to be shy."

Her father did something better—he stepped forward and hugged him. "We're happy to have you here with us."

"Geesh, thanks, Sir," Elf replied, surprised, and touched.

He glanced at his wife, silently asking if she'd had the talk with Elf.

"I told him, Honey," she confirmed with a smile.

Elf nodded. "Yes, Papa M. It'll take some getting used to, but I appreciate you both having me here."

"No more of that stranger-sounding talk," Mr. Madison said, clapping him gently on the back. "We're heading to my brother after dinner, so get cleaned up. Madds, you too—you know your uncle's a stickler for time."

"Yes Sir. I know," Mavis replied. "Dad, is the snowboarding arena open yet? I promised Elf, you'd take us."

"It opened last weekend. I drove past it the other morning—been excited for us to go. Patricia and Ethelyn might stop by for a day to meet Elf before you two head back, but no promises."

"That's fine. They spoke with him while we were waiting at the airport."

"Wonderful."

The ride to Uncle Adrian's house was filled with music and stories. Elf soaking in the warmth of the family he'd been folded into, sat in the back seat of the jeep with Mavis. The car smelled faintly of cedarwood and pine, and the windows fogged slightly from the cold outside. He watched the snow-covered trees blur past, feeling something, he hadn't felt in a long time—peace.

At Uncle Adrian's, the dogs greeted them like old friends, tails wagging and paws dancing. Uncle Adrian was loud and loving, his booming laugh echoing through the halls. He welcomed Elf with a hearty handshake and a wink. "Any friend of Madds is family here."

Later that night, as Elf lay in his new bed, surrounded by books and the soft hum of the house settling, he thought about the mystery they'd left behind. Dr. York. The pocket watch. The diary. It would all be waiting for them when they returned. But for now, he was home. And that was enough.

They made the most of their mid-term break— snowboarding at the indoor slopes arena, playing with Uncle Adrian's dogs, school shopping, and indulging in the all-you-can-eat buffet not once, but three times. The Madisons even took them camping near Mount Srice, where laughter echoed through the trees and stars blanketed the night sky. It was a week of joy, of forgetting the mystery and simply being present. Elf felt like family—because he was. And when they said Christmas was up to him, that he was always welcome, he believed them.

Chapter 22 – The Hot Chocolate Heist

The girls were back, the scent of cinnamon from someone's forgotten tea bag still lingering in the dorm air.

"I missed you, Cyn. How was Spikenard?" Mavis asked, arms outstretched.

Cyn hugged her tightly. "It was wonderful—my own bed, my mum's cooking, and Tim wasn't as annoying, which was a miracle. And Elf—did he enjoy being home with you and your family?"

She flopped onto her bed, while Mavis perched on the windowsill, legs swinging.

"We had a blast. My dad loved having him around for father-son stuff. Mum was thrilled too. He met my uncle and his dogs, we snowboarded, ate way too much ....It was perfect. He's welcome to come for Christmas if he wants."

Cyn tilted her head. "What about his parents? Won't they want him home for Christmas?"

Mavis shrugged. "It's up to them. We extended the invitation, but it's his choice."

"I just think everyone should be with their own family for Christmas," Cyn said softly. "His mum will want him home, Madison."

Mavis lowered her gaze. "Yeah   family is important. Christmas is for family." She looked up, her voice firmer. "But Elf is family to us too. If he wants to be with us, we'll make room."

Cyn gave a half-smile. "Well, I hope he goes home to his own family. Anyway—gifts!"

Mavis clapped. "I brought gifts for you too! Aww, we think alike."

They dove into their suitcases.

"Okay," Cyn said, "same time. On the count of three. One... two. ..three!"

"Oh, my goodness, I love these!" Mavis squealed, holding up a diary and a pair of espadrilles. "Are these from Spikenard?"

"Yup. Everything's local—even the paper for your diary. I figured you needed one of your own instead of just Maeve Brynn's."

"You're the best, Cyn. Do you like your gifts?"

"I love snow globes. I've ten on my dresser at home. They make me feel like I'm inside one—floating snow, frozen magic. And this t-shirt? Eli Garvon did a concert last summer in Spikenard!"

"No way! Get out!" Mavis laughed. "My sisters and I went to his concert two years ago. We've loved Eli Garvon forever."

A knock on the door interrupted their giggles.

"Hey neighbors!" Willow called, stepping in. "How was midterm break?"

"Great!" they chorused.

"Well, mine was spectacular. I shopped with my cousins and binged my favorite shows. Madison, did Elf go home with you?"

"He did—and we had a blast."

"Awesomeness. Toppy's back tomorrow," Willow said.

"The Garage opens tomorrow," Cyn added, rubbing her stomach. "And I'm starving."

"We could go to the kitchen and grab snacks. Maybe hot chocolate?" Willow suggested.

"The kitchen?" Cyn raised an eyebrow.

"Yeah. Toppy and I go there all the time for hot chocolate."

"How do you even get hot chocolate from the kitchen?" Cyn asked, suspicious.

"We do a heist," Willow grinned. "We squeeze our hands through the crack between the double fridge doors."

"Not for me," Cyn said flatly. "Besides I am allergic to chocolate remember."

"I brought back snacks and treats from home, if you'd like." Mavis offered.

"What do you have?" Willow asked as Mavis made her way to her trunk.

Rifling through it listing off various foods, "peanut butter, cassava chips, cans of spaghetti, guava sauce, "digging deeper, "I also have packs of Jammin' noodles and oh, a stack of granola bars and O'Henry chocolate bars."

"I could use a pack of Jammin' but we can still get some hot chocolate as well." She insisted.

"Okay." Said Mavis. "Cyn are you coming, we may find something for you in the pantry, I know you are hungry as well."

Cyn rolled her eyes. "Only because I'm hungry. I'm no thief—just putting that out there."

Willow laughed. "Neither are we. Just hungry girls on a cocoa mission."

"Let's go then," Mavis said, hopping off the windowsill.

"Quietly," Willow warned. "We don't want Biggertoe seeing us pass."

"It's not that late," Cyn muttered.

"Exactly," Willow whispered. "She thinks we're in our rooms. Let's keep it that way."

They giggled too loudly at first, passing packets of cocoa and marshmallows between them like they were top-secret. Willow's hand was wedged between the fridge doors, fingers curled around the last packet, then reaching for a juice box for Cyn and some hog plugs when—

"Shh!" Cyn hissed. "Someone's coming."

Willow froze, carefully withdrawing her hand. The three girls scrambled beneath the steel prep table, hearts thudding in sync. Mavis pressed her back against the cold metal, eyes wide. Footsteps echoed across the tile. Mavis squinted at the shoes—black leather, slightly scuffed at the toe. She knew those shoes anywhere.

"Menard," she mouthed.

Another pair joined her—sleek flats with a silver buckle. The voices drifted closer, then veered toward the far counter.

"I've finalized the menu," Menard said. "But we should include the rosemary rolls—his favorite."

"Agreed," the other woman replied. "And the lemon custard. He always said it reminded him of his grandmother's kitchen. A fitting tribute."

Menard sighed. "It's a shame things ended this way. He was reckless, always pushing boundaries. If only he'd left well enough alone. Still, the board approved everything. His name will be on the banners and flyers for the centennial ball. York would've liked that, I think."

The girls exchanged glances. Dr. York?

"We'll unveil the plaque during the closing ceremony," Menard added.

"A plaque?" Cyn whispered.

"We found a letter in the archives," the second woman said. "Written by Dr. York, sealed and marked 'To be opened upon my departure.'"

Mavis' breath caught.

"I just hope it doesn't mention that watch," Menard muttered. "We've kept up this sabbatical story long enough. We need to finish the tribute and lay his memory to rest. He's caused enough trouble. May he never darken these doors again."

Willow's eyes widened. Mavis leaned in, straining to hear.

"The pocket watch?" the second woman asked.

Menard nodded. "He called it 'a key to the past and a guide to the future.' Whatever that means."

The women moved toward the pantry, their voices fading.

Under the table, the girls sat frozen, with their loot close by.

"A key to the past?" Mavis whispered.

"And a guide to the future," Cyn echoed.

Willow grinned. "Looks like sleuthing season is officially back."

The kitchen was silent again. The women had left, their voices trailing off into the corridor. Mavis, Cyn, and Willow remained huddled beneath the steel table, hearts pounding.

"A plaque," Cyn whispered. "A sealed letter. And they don't want anyone asking about the watch?"

Mavis' mind raced. *A key to the past and a guide to the future.* That machine beneath the furnace. The message. The voice. They're hiding something," she said. "And it's connected to the machine."

Willow nodded. "We need to tell the others."

They slipped back to their dorm, cocoa packets in hand. Within minutes, Elf, Toppy, Kimp, Franny, Pierson, and Axton were gathered in their room, cross-legged on the floor, eyes wide – Axton and Pierson, continuing their game of jacks, Axton was winning.

"You're saying they found a letter?" Pierson asked, after scooping up his jacks, it was now Axton's turn.

"And they're planning a tribute," Cyn added. "But they don't want anyone asking about the watch."

Elf leaned forward. "That's strange. Especially since we know where it is."

Franny's eyes lit up. "The machine. Beneath the furnace."

"You found it?" Kimp asked, stunned.

Willow nodded. "Before midterm break. It's still running. A replica of the pocket watch is embedded in it."

"And it spoke," Mavis said quietly. "Dr. York's voice. He called me Miriam."

Axton whistled. "That's... wild."

Toppy frowned. "So, what now? Do we go back?"

"We have to," Mavis said. "If they're planning to read the letter, we need to know what really happened, and maybe we can save him, just maybe. Before they twist the story."

Elf stood. "Then we go tonight. But then we do have time, the ball is not until June and it's only the end of October."

"True." Mavis replied, "but I think unravelling what happened to him will take time and we need to get on this now."

Willow grinned. "Operation Furnace is back on."

Franny clapped her hands. "This is better than any mystery novel."

Mavis looked around at her friends—her team. The ones who believed in her, even when the truth felt too strange to speak aloud.

"Let's find out who Miriam really was," she said. "And why the machine thinks I'm her."

"That and more, "said Willow, "we have our chemistry teacher to save. Knowing Menard, he may be tied up in a damp basement."

Laughing, "for sure." Mavis agreed. "We just got back let us plan better, since Menard is still around tonight it may not be safe to go out. Let us go out another night."

"I did think, we were being too hasty." Said Cyn, "Menard and whomever the other lady was would surely see us. Menard is like the wind, she's everywhere."

"Agree." Said Franny, "she gives me the twitches, I am afraid of that woman."

The plan was simple: sneak out after lights-out, reach the furnace, re-enter the lab, decode the machine.

Simple... in theory.

But Thomas-Scott Academy had changed since midterm break. New locks sealed the basement doors. Motion sensors blinked in the east wing. And worst of all—Dean French now did nightly rounds, backed by a fresh security company.

"This is new," Pierson whispered as they crouched behind the library shelves, eyeing the patrols.

"Exactly," Mavis said. "Which means they know something—or they're hiding it."

"Vice Principal Ying's been acting strange too," Franny added. "He asked me if I'd seen any 'unauthorized tech' on campus."

"Unauthorized tech?" Elf repeated. "That's oddly specific."

"And Father Trent's last devotion was all about 'guarding the gates of knowledge,'" Willow said. "He stared right at me when he said it."

"So, we're surrounded by suspicious adults," Cyn muttered. "What else is new?"

They regrouped in the music room—neutral ground. The soft hum of the electric piano masked their whispers.

"We need a distraction," Axton said. "Something big enough to pull security from the east wing."

"I could trigger the fire alarm," Kimp offered.

"No," Mavis said. "Too risky. We need something subtle. Something... fun."

Franny grinned. "What if we host a midnight scavenger hunt? Blain mentioned at assembly that student council wanted event ideas."

"Perfect," Elf said. "We plant clues all over the west wing. They'll chase shadows while we slip into the basement."

"And we'll need disguises," Willow added. "If we get caught, we're just having fun on the hunt."

Mavis smiled. "Look at you all. My sleuths. Even Cyn's here."

"If you can't beat them, join them," Cyn said, sounding like an old soul.

"Blain sits at your table, Madison," Franny said. "Pitch the idea. Let us know if she's in."

"She'll love it," Willow said. "Who doesn't love a good scavenger hunt?"

The school's trip to the city aquarium was supposed to be educational. But when the tour guide began explaining the life of an octopus, Willow nudged Mavis. "Chocolate store. Two blocks away. You in?"

"Always." Leaning close to Cyn, "we are going to the chocolate store, you want to join us?"

"No, chocolate allergy, remember? And besides, we cannot leave now." The look of stress plastered across her forehead. "Madison...."

Swatting her hand dismissively, "I have seen enough fish to last a lifetime. This is so boring, 'the life of an octopus' I would rather hear about how snails eat through leaves." She whined, "we won't be long, a quick trip and before you know it, we will be back."

"You love stressing me, I am sure of it now."

"No, I don't you just like stressing."

"Is Cyn coming?" Willow asked, asked they both moved between their classmates going in the opposite direction from the view of the large fish tank.

"No, she's allergic to chocolate."

"That sucks." she remarked.

They grabbed Elf and slipped away, dodging chaperones and darting through alleyways. The store was heaven—walls of truffles, fountains of fudge.

"This beats the aquarium," Elf declared.

But just as they were paying, Mavis spotted a familiar silhouette outside.

"Menard," she whispered. "What is she doing here? She's like a booger that I cannot flick from finger." She whined.

They ducked behind a display of caramel turtles.

Dr. York & the Pocket Watch

"She's looking this way," Willow hissed.

"Act natural," Elf said, stuffing a bonbon in his mouth.

Menard walked past, distracted by her phone.

"Too close," Mavis said, heart racing.

"Totally worth it," Willow replied, licking chocolate off her fingers.

An exhale of relief, "we had better head back." Said Mavis.

"Why can't fun last forever?" Elf complained.

Slipping back next to Cyn.

"How was the it?" She asked.

"It is a store that have everything that a chocolate lover can feast on. We didn't' want to leave." She confessed, "but we saw Menard."

"You love playing with fate, you must love the danger of being close to her grip." Cyn whispered.

"Actually, this time I was terrified."

"Good, now you will ease up on testing your luck. That woman is like a hound dog; she always finds her prey."

Chapter 23 – A Delay

Tonight, they gathered in Mavis and Cyn's room ahead of the scavenger hunt.

"We have to work smart," Mavis said. "We can't let anyone catch on to what we're really doing."

"We could always back out," Cyn offered quietly.

Willow gasped. "Nope. We're too close now. We have to save Dr. York."

"Are we delusional?" Cyn asked. "Can we really save him— or are we playing with a fire that'll consume us?"

"You and your dramatic analogies," Mavis teased.

"Oh, it's not drama. It's truth. We could all be expelled." She replied.

Kimp groaned. "You're always such a wet blanket. Can't you be optimistic for once?"

Mavis shoved him lightly. "Don't speak to Cyn like that. She's our voice of reason, and I appreciate her." She touched Cyn's shoulder. "If we get caught, I'll take the blame. You won't be expelled."

"No, Madison," Elf said. "We're a team. You're not taking the fall alone."

"Exactly, we are a team," Pierson added, looking around the room, then directly at Cyn.

Cyn nodded. "We all go. Not just you. But thank you—for sticking up for me."

"I'm sorry, Cyn," Kimp said, sheepish.

"Think nothing of it," she replied, cutting off his apology with a small smile.

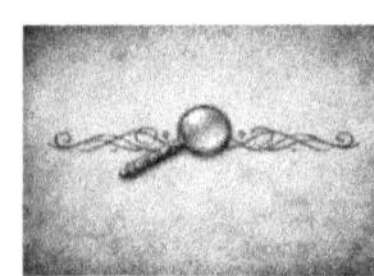

Midnight Scavenger Hunt: Operation Furnace Cover
Theme: *"Unlock the Secrets of Thomas-Scott"*
A playful nod to the school's history, with clues that feel like riddles but secretly help Mavis and her friends distract staff and security.

Dr. York & the Pocket Watch

The clock struck eleven. The halls of Thomas-Scott Academy were usually quiet at this hour, but not tonight. They were not. A shrill whistle echoed from the west wing, followed by the unmistakable sound of sneakers squeaking and students shrieking.

"It's on!" Pierson yelled, sprinting past the bulletin board with a flashlight taped to his forehead.

Franny darted behind him, clutching a clue card like it was the last golden ticket on Earth. "I found the note! It was behind the announcements about flu shots!"

In the art room, Kimp was halfway inside a supply cabinet, legs flailing. "Blue canvas, blue canvas—why are there so many shades of blue?!"

Willow, in oversized sunglasses and a trench coat, casually strolled past. "It's under the one with the angry duck. Obviously."

Meanwhile, Elf had turned the library into a war zone of whispers. "The book with the hollowed-out center is *not* in the mystery section. It's in poetry. Who hides chocolate in poetry?!"

"Someone with taste," Cyn muttered, flipping through titles like a caffeinated librarian.

At The Garage, students swarmed the counter, pretending to order cocoa while secretly reaching under the napkin dispenser. Toppy snagged the clue and did a victory dance that involved jazz hands and a pirouette.

"Subtle," Mavis said, watching from the shadows.

She, Willow, and Elf slipped away unnoticed, their disguises blending into the chaos. The scavenger hunt was working—security was distracted, staff were scrambling, and Dean French was yelling something about "unauthorized marshmallow activity."

In the greenhouse, Franny and Axton were elbow-deep in flowerpots.

"Forget-Me-Not!" Franny cried. "Found it!"

"Also found a worm," Axton said, grimacing. "Named him Reginald."

Back in the gym, Pierson opened a locker and screamed. "Spider!"

"It's fake," Cyn said, rolling her eyes. "But dramatic. I approve."

As the final clue was found, a hush fell over the crowd. Students gathered in the west wing, breathless and buzzing.

In the quiet that followed, she turned to Willow and Elf. "Ready?"

Willow pulled out her lock-picking kit. "Always."

They slipped into the east wing, hearts pounding, while the rest of the school celebrated their midnight victory.

The hunt was a success.

The hallway to the furnace room was darker than usual. The emergency lights flickered overhead, casting long, twitchy shadows on the walls. Mavis led the way; her flashlight dimmed to a whisper of light. Elf and Willow followed; lock-picking kit tucked in her hoodie pocket. Cyn trailed behind, she was curious, so she joined them, arms crossed tightly, eyes darting.

Willow reached the basement door and knelt beside the keypad. "Same encryption," she murmured. "I've got this."

But as she worked, a low hum filled the air. Not from the machine—but from somewhere else. A vibration. A presence.

Mavis froze. "Did you hear that?"

Elf nodded. "Like... footsteps?"

They turned. Nothing.

Cyn's breath hitched. "We're going to get expelled. I can feel it. They'll find us, and we'll be toast. Burnt toast."

Willow paused, her fingers hovering over the lock. "I don't think we're alone."

They scanned the hallway. Empty.

Still, the feeling lingered—like someone was watching. Like the shadows were listening.

Mavis stepped back. "Let's not push it tonight."

Willow nodded. "Agreed. The locks aren't going anywhere."

They retreated, hearts pounding, nerves frayed.

Back in the dorm, Cyn collapsed onto her bed. "I swear I saw a figure. Tall. Like Father Trent, but... not."

"It was probably just nerves," Elf said. "Or a coat rack."

"Or a ghost," Franny added helpfully.

Dr. York & the Pocket Watch

Mavis sat by the window, staring out into the night. The machine was still a mystery. The letter, the plaque, the watch—it all pointed to something bigger.

Then a thought struck her.

"What if we find out where Dr. York lived?" she said. "Maybe there's something there. A clue. A journal. Something he left behind."

Willow perked up. "You mean... a field trip?"

"Exactly," Mavis said. "We find his house. We search it. Carefully."

Cyn groaned. "You people are allergic to rules."

Franny grinned. "And we're proud of it."

Mavis looked around at her crew. The mystery wasn't just beneath the furnace. It was everywhere. And they were just getting started.

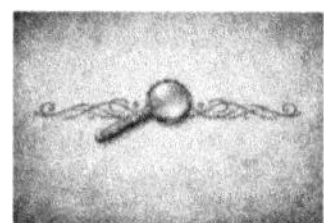

Assembly was in full swing. The headmaster droned on about academic excellence and the importance of proper sock length.

Pierson slipped out, clutching his stomach dramatically. "Bathroom emergency," he whispered to the nearest teacher, who waved him off with mild concern.

But the bathroom wasn't his destination. He detoured to the administrative office, where Ms. Dalloway, the secretary, sat typing furiously.

"Ms. Dalloway!" Pierson said, breathless. "I think someone spilled paint in the art room sink. It's clogging the drain and flooding the counter. I came straight here, because you are closest to the bathroom and I wanted to report it."

Ms. Dalloway blinked. "Paint? In the sink?"

"Bright orange. It's everywhere. I think it's acrylic. Or lava. Hard to tell."

She sighed, grabbed her keys, and muttered something about "art kids and their chaos" before heading off toward the east wing.

Pierson waited until her footsteps faded, then slipped behind the desk.

"Okay, York," he whispered. "Where did you live?"

He tapped into the staff database, bypassing the login with a trick Elf taught him involving the caps lock key and an admin shortcut. The screen blinked. Access granted.

He scrolled past cafeteria schedules, substitute lists, and a suspicious number of printer repair requests.

Then—bingo.

York, Dr. Sphinx Status: Sabbatical (Unverified) Last Known Address: 1127 Wren Hollow Lane. Unlisted. Hidden in a folder marked "Archived Personnel."

Pierson scribbled it down, cleared the browser history, and even left a sticky note on the desk that read: *"You're doing great, Ms. D!"*

He slipped back into assembly just as headmistress Menard was praising the virtues of punctuality.

Later that night, he handed the note to Mavis.

"Found him," he said. "And you owe me a stromboli from The Garage."

Mavis grinned. "You're brilliant."

"Obviously."

Chapter 24 – Truth has Teeth

The classroom lights flickered once, then dimmed to a soft hum. A shimmer of static danced above the teacher's desk before coalescing into the familiar form of Dr. Sphinx York—holographic, crisp, and unsettlingly lifelike.

He wore his usual tweed blazer, but today, the golden pocket watch glinted more brightly than usual, pulsing faintly with a rhythmic glow. It ticked audibly, though no one had ever heard it tick before.

York's gaze swept the room, pausing—too long—on Mavis, Elf, and Willow. His eyes narrowed, as if he could see through their thoughts and into the folder marked "Archived Personnel."

"Pop quiz," he said, voice clipped. "No notes. No excuses."

The questions appeared instantly on their tablets. Complex chemical equations, obscure compound identifications, and one cryptic question: **"What binds the invisible to the real?"**

York didn't pace. He sat—cross-legged—on the desk, watching them. Not the way a teacher watches for cheating. The way a detective watches for guilt.

Mavis' pen trembled slightly. Elf muttered something about "quantum weirdness." Willow scribbled furiously; her brow furrowed.

When the timer beeped, York vanished the quiz with a flick of his wrist. "Dismissed," he said. "Except for Madison."

The others hesitated, but Mavis nodded. "It's okay," she whispered.

York's hologram didn't flicker. It leaned forward.

"You've seemed... distracted," he said. "Your focus has waned. Chemistry requires precision."

"I'm not distracted," Mavis replied, steady but respectful. "I've been focused. I got all the quiz questions right."

York tilted his head. "Indeed. But correctness is different from clarity."

The pocket watch ticked louder.

"I hope," he added, "you're not chasing ghosts."

Mavis swallowed. "I'm chasing truth."

York's image paused, then gave the faintest smile. "Be careful. Truth has teeth."

The bell rang, but the air didn't clear. Mavis stepped into the hallway, her mind still echoing with York's words: "Truth has teeth."

It gnawed at her. Not just the phrase, but the way he said it—like he knew something she didn't. Like he wasn't warning her but daring her.

Her friends were waiting just outside the door, clustered near the lockers. Elf was pacing. Willow clutched her sketchbook like a shield. Toppy had her hoodie pulled tight, eyes darting between Mavis and the classroom.

"You okay?" Franny asked, voice low.

Mavis nodded, but it was the kind of nod that meant *not really*.

"We heard him," Cyn said. "That was... intense."

"He's never like that," Willow added. "Even when he's glitchy, he's not that sharp."

"He looked right at us," Elf muttered. "Like he knew we were digging."

Mavis leaned against the wall, the coolness grounding her. "He said truth has teeth."

"What does that even mean?" Toppy asked.

"It means," Cyn said, "maybe we should take a break. Finals are coming up. We're all stretched thin."

There was a pause. The kind that happens when no one wants to agree, but no one wants to argue either.

"I don't know," Mavis said finally. "It's not just about York anymore. It's about what he's hiding. That watch—it was glowing. And that quiz? One of the questions wasn't even chemistry."

Elf perked up. "You mean the invisible-real one?"

"Exactly. He's testing us. Not just academically."

Willow frowned. "So, what do we do?"

Mavis looked at her friends—each one anxious, loyal, and tangled in this mystery with her.

"We breathe," she said. "We prep for finals. But we don't stop. Not completely."

Cyn sighed. "Half-speed sleuthing. I can live with that."

"Truth has teeth," Elf repeated. "Well, so do we."

They all smiled at that. Even Mavis.

The library smelled like old paper and peppermint gum—someone had snuck in candy canes again. Mavis, Elf, Willow, Toppy, Cyn, Axton, Franny, Pierson, and Kimp had claimed their usual corner table beneath the tall arched window, where the afternoon light slanted in like a spotlight on their chaos. Books were stacked like barricades. Highlighters squeaked. Someone's phone buzzed with a lo-fi study playlist. And in the middle of it all, a small drawing of Dr. York's pocket watch sat between their notebooks, sketched by Willow in the margins of her Lit notes.

"I still think the watch is the key," Elf said, tapping it with his pencil. "It glowed. That's not normal."

"Neither is a hologram teacher assigning pop quizzes with existential riddles," Toppy muttered, flipping through *Lord of the Flies*. "Ms. Petty basically wants us to write our dissertations. I'm only eleven. I still eat cereal for dinner."

Willow groaned. "Can we not talk about York for five minutes? I'm running on candy and fear. Finals are next week. I haven't even cracked *The Color Purple*."

"Same," Cyn said. "And don't forget the gift exchange. We still have to shop."

Pierson perked up. "Shopping weekend. Downtown. Shuttle leaves Saturday at ten. We could swing by Wren Hollow Lane..."

"Nope," Willow said, firm. "New year. I vote we sleuth after finals. I want to survive long enough to open presents."

Franny nodded. "Seconded. I already wrapped mine. I got someone who's impossible to shop for."

"Who?" Kimp asked.

Franny smirked. "Not telling."

They all laughed, the tension easing for a moment.

Then Elf went quiet. He was staring at his untouched notes, fingers curled around his pen. "My dad wants me home for Christmas," he said finally. "He never asks. Not since... not since Mum."

The table stilled.

"He said he and my stepmum are 'trying.' Whatever that means. I don't know. It feels weird. Like a setup."

Cyn gave Mavis a look. "Told you. Christmas is for family."

She gave a faint smile. Then she looked at Elf reminding him that no one knows of his mum's passing but her, and yet he's about to tell them something he told her to keep private. He understood her protection of the secret, but he's good and they have shown to be his true friends. He nodded, as if giving her permission; giving himself permission to share something so painful.

He continued, "Yeah, but they haven't acted like family in years."

Mavis reached across the table and squeezed his hand. "The invitation's still open. If you need to, you know you can come home with me. My parents already asked if you were coming. You're family, Elf. Always."

His eyes shimmered, just a little. "Thanks, Madison."

"Don't get sappy," Pierson said, tossing a candy cane at him. "You're ruining my brooding."

They all laughed again, softer this time. The kind of laugh that comes when you're tired, but safe. When the world is strange, but your people are close.

Outside, the sun was setting.

The shuttle dropped them off at the edge of the town square, where palm trees were strung with fairy lights and a steel drum band played a calypso version of "Jingle Bells." The breeze off the sea carried the scent of salt and sugar, and the sun glinted off the tinsel-wrapped lampposts. Mavis stepped off first, her canvas tote slung over her shoulder, already half-filled with allergy medicine, and band-aids . Elf followed, humming along to the music, while Toppy adjusted her sling shoulder bag and declared, "This is the only kind of winter I'll ever accept." Bell ringers in red polos and Santa hats stood outside every shop, their cheerful chimes blending with the laughter of children and the occasional bark of a dog in a holiday sweater.

They wandered in and out of quaint boutiques—shops with names like *The Coral Quill* and *Seashell & Sage.* In one, they found hand-bound journals with covers made from pressed seaweed and recycled driftwood. Each of them picked one out for their gift exchange recipient, even though none of them had drawn each other's names.

"I got someone named Lyle," Mavis said, inspecting a journal with a compass etched into the cover. "I think he's in eighth grade, or maybe ninth."

"I got a girl named Priya," Willow said. "She's in my art class. She paints clouds that look like emotions."

"I got a kid who once asked if glue was edible," Pierson muttered. "He's getting a journal and a warning label."

They stopped at *Café Marisol,* where the windows were fogged with steam and the air smelled like cinnamon and citrus. Mavis ordered hot chocolate with extra whipped cream. Elf got the same, while Cyn, being allergic to chocolate, ordered her favorite—warm milk with nutmeg and a thick slice of spiced currant cake.

"This is heaven," Cyn said, sipping contentedly. "No stress, just sugar and sea air."

"I wish we could stay here forever," Elf said, watching the waves roll in just beyond the boardwalk. "Or at least until finals are over."

Mavis smiled. "We'll survive. And then we'll sleuth."

"After Christmas," Willow reminded them. "We promised."

They all nodded, the promise unspoken but understood. For now, it was about peppermint-scented sidewalks, carolers in flip-flops, and the joy of giving—even if they secretly hoped for something more exciting than a journal in return. As the sun dipped lower, casting golden light across the ocean, they posed for a group photo in front of a sand-sculpted snowman wearing sunglasses and holding a candy cane surfboard.

"Say 'coconut custard pie!'" Toppy called.

"Coconut custard pie!" they chorused, laughing as the camera clicked.

Just as they finished their drinks, a group of carolers in flip-flops and hibiscus-print shirts burst into the café, singing "Deck the Halls" with ukuleles and maracas. Elf clapped along, while Toppy tried to harmonize and accidentally knocked over a sugar shaker. The café owner, a cheerful woman with a parrot on her shoulder, waved it off with a wink and handed them each a peppermint lollipop shaped like a seashell.

Outside, the square had transformed into a pop-up holiday carnival. Mavis spotted a booth offering "Snowball Toss" with coconut husks and a prize wheel shaped like a sand dollar. Pierson won a tiny plush manatee wearing a Santa hat, which he immediately named "Professor Blub." Then came the impromptu limbo contest under a string of twinkling lights. Cyn, surprisingly flexible, made it to the final round before losing to a local kid in sparkly swim trunks.

"I demand a rematch," she declared, laughing as she accepted a consolation prize—a glittery sticker that read *Limbo Legend in Training.'*

They were so caught up in the festivities that none of them noticed the time until a loudspeaker crackled overhead: "Final shuttle to Thomas-Scott Academy departs in five minutes."

"Five minutes?" Mavis yelped, grabbing her tote. "We're on the other side of the square!"

What followed was a chaotic dash—dodging stilt walkers dressed as candy canes, weaving through a conga line of tourists, and hurdling over a sand sculpture of a reindeer. Elf nearly tripped over a ukulele case, and Franny lost her flip-flop mid-sprint, retrieving it with a dramatic dive that earned applause from a nearby mime. They reached the shuttle just as the doors began to close. Toppy flung herself forward, wedging her sling bag between the doors like a heroic movie stunt. The driver sighed and reopened them with a muttered, "Teenagers."

Inside the shuttle, Headmistress Menard stood with arms crossed and eyebrows raised so high they nearly touched her hairline. "I trust you all had a *productive* afternoon," she said, her voice clipped and cool.

"Yes, ma'am," they chorused, breathless and grinning.

"Let's hope your finals are approached with the same enthusiasm," she added, settling into her seat with a pointed glance. "Because if I see one more glitter sticker on the floor of this shuttle, someone's getting detention."

Cyn discreetly peeled hers off her arm and tucked it into her journal.

Chapter 25 – Friendships Tested

The next morning, finals began.

Mavis' alarm blared with unnatural cheer. She swatted it like a fly, sending it tumbling onto a heap of books. She slid out of bed and knelt to pray. As she rose, she noticed Cyn's bed was empty. The shower was running. She grabbed her uniform and rummaged for undergarments. Cyn emerged, towel-wrapped and wide-eyed.

"I've been up since 4:30," Cyn said. "Math equations bouncing around my brain. I hope I remember what goes on the left and what goes on the right. Why do we even need math? It should be an elective."

Mavis laughed. "You worry too much. You've studied. You'll do fine. Now let me shower before Toppy beats me to it."

But the water started again.

"She beat me," Mavis groaned, flopping onto Cyn's bed. "I love her, but she takes forever."

"That's why I went first," Cyn said smugly.

Assembly dragged on. Principal Menard spoke. Dean French issued a stern warning about cheating. Father Trent offered a mercifully short prayer. Deputy Headmaster Ying dismissed them.

Thirty minutes until exams. Mavis flipped through her chemistry notes. First up: Dr. York.

At 9:00 sharp, he arrived—dressed like a holiday fever dream in a red herringbone coat and velvet green pants. Willow did a double take.

"Good morning, my favorite students," he said. "I trust you're ready to ace your chemistry exam. I won't repeat Dean French's warning, but do be aware... Now, let's begin."

Elf made the sign of the cross.

"This isn't church, Edward," Dr. York said dryly. "No need for theatrics."

Elf flushed.

The exam appeared on their tablets. Mavis kept her eyes glued to the screen, avoiding York's gaze. She just wanted to get through it. The ticking of the pocket watch synced eerily with the exam timer. The questions were brutal. Mavis blinked at one. Was this for seventh grade or eleventh? The ticking grated on her nerves, but she pressed on.

Ding.

"Stop," York bellowed.

Mavis exhaled for the first time in an hour.

"You're bright students," he said. "I won't see you before the holidays, so I wish you a safe one. It's been a pleasure teaching you." Then: "Madison, Edward, Willow—stay behind."

Whispers erupted. *Why them?*

York waited until the room cleared.

"You're my top three," he said. "Edward, your improvement has been remarkable. Willow and Madison, you're neck and neck. Madison, your mother would be proud."

"Thank you, Dr. York," they chorused.

"That will be all." He turned to the window, then back. "Truth has teeth."

He left.

Elf whispered, "He knows."

Willow's eyes widened. "I felt it. He knows. What now, Madison? Will he haunt us?"

"He's not a ghost," Mavis said. "Someone's programming him—or maybe he's doing it himself. I think he wants us to find out. Maybe he's warning us to be careful."

"We have to tell the others," Elf said.

"Wait," Willow said. "How did he know what Dean French said at assembly?"

"She just started this year," Mavis said. "He shouldn't know."

"Exactly," Willow said. "We'll update the others at lunch. But no sleuthing until after recess. I want a peaceful Christmas break."

"Agreed," Mavis said. "Just a quick update."

Mavis and Cyn were practically vibrating with excitement. Christmas was their season—the lights, the music, the peppermint everything. And today, the last day of school. No uniforms. No exams. Just pure, unfiltered festivity: caroling, feasting, and exchanging gifts.

The dorm was buzzing. Students zipped around in holiday sweaters and fuzzy socks, laughter echoing down the halls. Mavis was on a mission—digging through her closet for the perfect sweater to match her red jeans. Cyn, meanwhile, was bouncing on her heels, clutching her phone like it was a golden ticket.

"Xandria's returning!" Cyn squealed.

Mavis didn't look up. She was elbow-deep in knitwear.

"Did you hear me?" Cyn asked, peering over Mavis' shoulder.

"I heard you," Mavis said, taking out a sweater with a dancing Santa stitched across the front. "I'm just trying to find something festive that doesn't make me look like a candy cane."

Cyn crossed her arms. "I know you don't like her."

Mavis shrugged. "I don't despise her. But let's be honest— the feeling's mutual."

"Are you worried she'll take your place?"

Mavis frowned. "Why would I think that? We don't click. And honestly, I think she's jealous of our friendship."

"She's not," Cyn said, a little too quickly. "She's a good friend. I just hope you two can get along—for my sake. I haven't seen her since September."

Mavis held up the Santa sweater triumphantly. "Found it!"

Cyn groaned. "Madison, are you even listening?"

"Yes," Mavis said, "you want me and Xandria to get along. Got it. But really, Cyn, it's not that deep. If you want to hang out with her, go for it. It doesn't change us. I've got Elf and the others."

Cyn muttered under her breath, "Yes, Elf. Your best friend."

Mavis caught it. "He's not. He's, my brother. Totally different category."

"No, it's not," Cyn argued. "My sisters are best friends and siblings."

Dr. York & the Pocket Watch

"Well, Elf is my brother, and you're my best friend. The lines aren't blurred. Now, if I don't get in the shower before Toppy, I'll be waiting till New Year's."

She darted out of the room, knocking on the bathroom door shared with Toppy and Willow. "In the shower!" she called.

"You beat me!" Toppy shouted. "Leave the water running when you're done!"

"Will do!" Mavis shouted back.

Willow was still asleep, having binged her favorite show until the wee hours. She'd asked Toppy to wake her once the bathroom cleared. Tomorrow, she'd be heading home—and she was already dreaming of her mum's cranberry scones.

By 8:30, the girls were dressed and glowing, gifts in hand and holiday spirit in full swing. Breakfast was a dream: cinnamon and vanilla French toast topped with eggnog whipped cream, scrambled eggs, sausage links, and a choice of milk or tea. There was even a station for seasonal fruits and another for chicken souse.

Cyn and Willow went back for seconds. Cyn declared it "the best breakfast of the semester," mouth full of toast.

But one person was missing.

Mavis scanned the room, her eyes landing on the empty seat where Elf usually sat. She pulled out her phone.

> **Mavis:** *Why aren't you at breakfast? Are you okay?*
> **Elf:** *Still packing.*
> **Mavis:** *Are you coming to breakfast?*
> **Elf:** *No. I'll see you at assembly.*
> **Mavis:** *Elf, I know you don't want to go home, but maybe it won't be so bad.*
> **Elf:** *I honestly don't want to go home. But... I have to.*
> **Mavis:** *We'll talk at assembly.*

The assembly hall was a kaleidoscope of color and sound, transformed into a winter wonderland. Dean French and Miss Saltz had gone all out decorating since early December. Garlands draped the walls, twinkling lights framed the stage, and the air smelled like cinnamon, cardamom, vanilla, and cloves. Mavis and Cyn skipped in together, practically glowing. Willow, Axton, Pierson, Franny, Toppy, and Elf arrived chatting and laughing. Mavis' heart lifted when she saw Elf smiling—he'd been quiet lately, dreading the trip home to his father and stepmother. But today, he looked lighter.

They sat together, singing carols and swaying to the music.

Mavis glanced at Elf, who was watching Menard with a bemused smile. She nudged him gently. "You okay?"

He nodded. "Better now."

The music swelled—"Rockin' Around the Christmas Tree"—and Headmistress Menard took the stage in a glittery red blazer, dancing with surprising rhythm. The students erupted in cheers.

"She's definitely had spiked eggnog," Pierson whispered.

"Or she's finally letting loose," Kimp replied, grinning.

Willow could not believe it, *could Menard actually be human?* She thought to herself.

The gift exchange began in a flurry of wrapping paper and squeals. Students darted around, trying to find their Secret Santa recipients. Willow handed a hand-bound journal to a shy seventh grader named Priya, who gasped and hugged her. Pierson gave his recipient a journal and a sticker that read *"Not for eating."* Cyn received a sketchbook with her name etched in gold foil

Then came the moment Cyn had been waiting for.

Xandria walked in, she had been doing school online since the end of September – a family matter pulled her out from school, but she will return in the new year. She wore a sleek emerald dress and a gold velvet headband, her curls bouncing as she moved. The room seemed to pause for half a second. Cyn squealed and ran to hug her.

"You're here!" Cyn cried. "I missed you so much!"

"I missed you too," Xandria said, squeezing her tightly. "It's been awful being away. But I'm back now."

Mavis watched from across the room, her smile polite but tight. Willow leaned in.

"She's got that look," Willow whispered. "Like she's sizing up the competition."

"She's always had that look," Mavis replied.

Cyn pulled Xandria over to the group. "Everyone, you remember Xandria!"

"Hey," Xandria said, her voice smooth as silk. "Nice to see you all again."

"Welcome back," Elf said, offering a nod.

Willow gave a small wave. Toppy smiled, but her eyes flicked to Mavis.

Xandria looped her arm through Cyn's and leaned in. "I've got so much to tell you. Let's catch up—just us."

Mavis felt the shift. The way Xandria angled her body, the way she spoke only to Cyn, the way she didn't even glance at the others. It was subtle, but it was there.

Cyn hesitated. "We're all hanging out together, though. Right?"

Xandria's smile faltered for a fraction of a second. "Of course. I just meant... later."

Mavis turned away, pretending to adjust her gift bag. Willow nudged her gently. "She wants Cyn all to herself," she murmured.

"I know," Mavis said. "But Cyn's not a prize to be won."

The rest of the morning passed in a blur of carols, cocoa, and laughter. Mavis stayed close to Elf, who seemed grateful for the distraction. Cyn bounced between her two worlds— trying to include everyone, trying to keep the peace.

But Mavis saw it. The way Xandria whispered in Cyn's ear. The way she rolled her eyes when Mavis spoke. The way she clung a little too tightly.

Later, as they packed for break, Mavis sat on her bed, folding sweaters and humming softly. Cyn walked in, holding a small, wrapped box.

"This is for you," she said. "From me. Not Secret Santa. Just... me."

Mavis opened it. Inside was a charm bracelet with tiny silver books and a heart-shaped locket.

"I love it," Mavis said, touched. "Thank you."

"I know today was weird," Cyn said. "But you're my best friend. That hasn't changed."

Mavis smiled. "I know. And I'm not worried. I just hope she knows that too."

Chapter 26 – Melancholy yet Sweet

The shuttle ride to the airport was quieter than usual. Mavis and Elf sat side by side, their bags tucked between their knees, watching the island blur past the windows. The others had left earlier or were catching later flights, but the two of them had chosen to ride together—just like they had during midterm break. Back then, Elf had flown home with Mavis, spent the week with her family, played with her Uncle Adrian's dogs, snowboarded, shopped, and ate more than they should have — it had been warm and chaotic and full of laughter. Mavis had loved every second of it. So had Elf.

Now, the mood was different.

"I wish you were coming with me again," Mavis said softly.

Elf looked out the window. "Me too."

They didn't say much after that. They didn't need to. The silence between them was familiar, like a well-worn blanket—comfortable, but heavy.

At the airport, they walked together through the terminal, dodging rolling suitcases, and families in matching pajamas. Mavis' gate was to the left. Elf's was to the right.

They stopped at the fork in the corridor.

"This is it," Elf said, adjusting the strap on his backpack.

Mavis nodded, trying to smile. "Three weeks. Then we're back. Sleuthing. Pocket watch. The diary. Dr. York."

Elf chuckled. "And cafeteria mystery meat."

She stepped forward and hugged him tightly. He hugged back, longer than usual.

"I'll miss you," she whispered.

"I'll miss you more," he said. "Promise me you'll text me every day."

"Only if you promise to answer." She replied.

They pulled apart slowly. Elf's eyes were glassy, but he blinked it away.

"Go," he said. "Before I change my mind and sneak onto your flight."

Mavis laughed, but it was soft and sad.

They waved once more before turning toward their gates. Mavis didn't look back. She knew if she did, she'd cry. And she wanted Elf to remember her smiling.

Dr. York & the Pocket Watch

Christmas Eve had always carried a bittersweet hum for Elf. But this year, the sweetness had been scraped away entirely, leaving only the hollow echo of what used to be. He sat stiffly on the edge of the leather couch in his father's study, the fire crackling behind him, casting flickering shadows across the mahogany walls.

His father stood by the window, swirling a glass of something amber, his tone clipped and clinical. "We're moving to Indonesia," he said, as if announcing a quarterly earnings report. "The market's ripe. The expansion will be massive. Your stepmother's thrilled."

Elf blinked. "Okay."

"And we're selling the house," his father added. "It's too much to maintain from overseas."

That was the blow. Not the move. Not the business. But the house. The only home Elf had ever known. The place where his mother had read him bedtime stories, where they'd baked banana bread on rainy Sundays, where her laughter still lingered in the corners of the kitchen. Selling it felt like erasing her. Like erasing him.

"And you'll be staying with Fred," his father continued. "He's agreed to be your guardian. We'll sign the papers the day after Christmas."

Elf nodded. He didn't cry. His father didn't allow tears. He'd learned to save them for the dark, for the silence, for the moments when no one was watching.

That night, in the privacy of his room, he texted Mavis.

Elf: *My dad's selling the house. They are moving to Indonesia. I'm being signed over to Uncle Fred the day after Christmas.*

Mavis: *What? Elf, I'm so sorry. That house... it's your whole childhood.*

Elf: *He said it's not personal. Just logistics.*

Mavis: *I'm telling my parents. Hold on.*

Within fifteen minutes, Mavis had gathered her parents in the living room, her voice trembling as she explained. Her mother's eyes welled with tears. Her father paced, then stopped suddenly.

"If Elf's father agrees," Mr. Madison said, "we'll take guardianship. No charge. He can live with us, visit Indonesia when needed. We'll make it work."

Mavis texted again.

Mavis: *Tell your dad. My parents want to be your guardians. You'll stay with us. You'll be safe.*

Elf stared at the message for a long time. Then, with a deep breath, he walked back into the study. "Dad," he said. "Madison's parents want to be my guardians. They're offering stability. No cost. I'd like that, may I stay with them instead?"

His father looked surprised. Then relieved. "That might be better," he said. "Fred's not exactly... equipped. I'll have the notary come in three days. Mr. Madison can make the trip over from Coco Plum Cay. I'll speak with the Madisons—I have their number." He turned back to his drink. "Now off to bed. We have early mass and lunch with one of your stepmother's former colleagues."

"Merry Christmas, Dad," Elf said quietly.

The room was cold—not from the weather, but from the absence of love. Love had left the day his mother died. But on the bright side, Elf would be with Mavis and her family. They were warm. They were real. And this was already the best Christmas he'd had in years.

Two days after Christmas, Mr. Madison flew in. The notary met them at the local library. Papers were signed. Mr. Farrington and Mr. Madison shook hands like they'd just closed a business deal. Elf watched the ink dry, feeling something shift inside him—something like hope.

Mr. Madison clapped a hand on his shoulder. "You're part of our family now. No matter what."

Elf nodded, swallowing the lump in his throat. "Thank you."

He glanced at his father and stepmother. They looked more relieved than emotional. He wondered if they'd ever ask him to visit Indonesia. His gut said no. This might be the last time he saw his father.

"Well, Elf," his father said, voice flat as a soda fizz. "You can stay here until school resumes or go back with Mr. Madison. Your choice."

Elf looked at Mr. Madison, trying not to seem too eager.

"My wife and I would love for you to come," Mr. Madison said gently. "If you're ready to say goodbye for now."

"Yes, sir," Elf replied, lowering his eyes so his father wouldn't see the flicker of joy in them.

"Then it's settled. I'll purchase your ticket," his father said. "Mr. Madison, you're welcome to stay at our home tonight before your flight. It's the least I can do."

"Elf is no imposition," Mr. Madison replied. "We love having him. My girls adore him."

His father gave a faint smile that never reached his eyes.

The next morning, Elf and his father exchanged farewells.

"Don't forget your manners at the Madisons," his father said. "Earn your keep. Help where needed. I'll see you once we're settled."

He turned to Mr. Madison. "Please thank your lovely wife. I appreciate your family boarding my son."

"We love having him," Mr. Madison said. "Thank you for trusting us."

Then, unexpectedly, his father pulled Elf into a brief squeeze. "Elf, I love you."

Elf froze. His father had never said that before. He didn't know how to respond. "Yes, sir," was all he could manage.

His stepmother hugged him, but it felt like a formality. No warmth. No weight.

Mr. Madison and Elf took a taxi to the airport. Elf didn't want his father driving him—not today. Mrs. Madison and Mavis were waiting at the terminal. Mr. Madison waved the signed papers in the air like a victory flag.

"We have a son," he said, kissing his wife's cheek.

Mavis ran to Elf and hugged him tight. He cried.

"Thank you for rescuing me," he whispered.

"We're family," she said. "This is your family."

They skipped, then raced to the car. Elf was home. He was safe. He was loved. The rest of the holiday was filled with introductions to extended family, laughter at parties, and quiet moments of peace.

On New Year's Eve, his father called from Indonesia. "We've landed safely," he said. "Happy New Year. All the best at school."

Elf thanked him. But he didn't feel tossed aside anymore. He felt chosen.

Chapter 27 - Forgiveness

The first day after break felt like Christmas eve again — the courtyard buzzed with laughter, hugs, and overlapping stories as students reunited, their voices rising like birdsongs. Mavis and Elf walked in together, side by side, their steps light and their smiles wide. Mr. Madison had already scanned and emailed the signed guardianship papers to the school office, ensuring Elf's records were updated before school started. The subject line read: *"Guardianship Confirmation – Edward Loftus Farrington (Elf)"* and the message was simple: *"To whom it may concern, the following attachment is the paperwork, signing guardianship of Edward Loftus Farrington by Mr. Theophilus Lynx Farrington to Mr. Xion Madison and Mrs. Mavis Evelyn Madison, Sr., Edward is now in our care and any matters pertaining to him our contact is listed. Thank you."*

At the courtyard, their friends were already gathered—Cyn, Willow, Pierson, Kimp, Franny, Toppy, and Axton— huddled together bouncing with excitement.

"Madison!" Cyn shouted, launching into a hug. "You're back! I missed you so much." Then hugging Elf, "you look happy." She said.

"I am very happy," Elf said. "Like someone took a backpack full of bricks off my shoulders."

Mavis beamed. "He's officially part of our family now."

"You're a Madison?" Franny gasped.

"Well sort of, the Madisons are my guardians, my father moved to Indonesia."

"That's so cool. I think you should change your name to 'Madison'." She added.

"My dad would implode, if I did that."

They all laughed, then the chatter continued, conversations overlapping:

"I went sledding with my cousins and crashed into a snowman!" "My grandma gave me a mystery novel with a secret code in the margins!" "I got socks. Again. But they have magnifying glasses on them this time." "I learned how to make peppermint bark and burned my eyebrows off!"

Then Axton stepped forward, holding a large box wrapped in newspaper comics. "I figured we'd need these," he said, opening the box with a flourish. Inside were nine pairs of sleek, compact binoculars—each one engraved with their initials and a tiny magnifying glass symbol. "For sleuthing," Axton said. "Because we're not just friends. We're investigators."

The group erupted in cheers.

"This is amazing!" Willow said, adjusting hers and scanning the courtyard like a spy.

"I feel like a detective-slash-birdwatcher," Pierson added.

Mavis hugged Axton. "You're the best. Seriously."

"I know," he said with a sheepish smile. "But I would prefer chocolates over compliments."

They spent the rest of the morning swapping stories, testing their binoculars, and planning their next mystery meeting. Elf sat beside Mavis; his heart full. He wasn't just back—he was home.

Xandria's return to campus after the holiday break stirred more than excitement—it stirred old tensions. She had barely unpacked before suggesting that Cyn move into her room, and that her current roommate moves in with Mavis. The request was casual on the surface, but the intent was clear. Xandria wanted Cyn all to herself.

Cyn hesitated, then stood her ground. "Mavis is my best friend," she said firmly. "We can be friends too, but you have to respect that."

Xandria's smile faltered. "I just thought we'd reconnect. Things were different before."

But Cyn saw through it. The jealousy was still there, simmering beneath Xandria's polished exterior. Later that evening, Xandria pressed harder, asking about the group's activities. Cyn, caught between loyalty and nostalgia, shared more than she should have—details about their investigation into Dr. York and the pocket watch. She made Xandria promise not to tell anyone.

Dr. York & the Pocket Watch

What Cyn didn't know was that Xandria had no intention of keeping that promise. She didn't like Mavis. Never had. She found her too self-assured, too quick to lead, too confident in her opinions. And more than anything, she wanted Cyn's friendship back—exclusively.

When the others found out what Cyn had shared, the reaction was swift and sharp. Willow was stunned. Pierson was furious. Even Elf, usually calm, looked betrayed. They had a code—what was shared in the group stayed in the group. Cyn had broken that.

Cyn tried to explain. "I didn't mean any harm. I just thought I could trust her."

Mavis, ever composed, stepped forward. "I'm not worried about Xandria. She doesn't scare me. But Cyn... you should've known better."

Cyn's eyes welled with tears. "I'm sorry. I really am."

The group didn't respond right away. The silence was heavy. But then Mavis spoke again, her voice softer. "We all make mistakes. What matters is what we do next."

It wasn't forgiveness—not yet. But it was a start.

Later, Mavis pulled Cyn aside. "You're still my best friend," she said. "But trust is earned. Let's rebuild it—together."

Cyn nodded, grateful and ashamed. She knew it would take time. She knew the others might not confide in her the same way again. But she also knew she'd fight to earn it back.

As for Xandria, her plan to isolate Mavis had failed. The group was shaken but not broken. And Mavis? She stood taller than ever, her leadership tested and proven.

Cyn had been quiet since the fallout. She kept her head down in study hall, skipped lunch with the group, and barely spoke during their sleuthing sessions. The sting of broken trust lingered, and though Mavis had extended grace, the others weren't ready to forget.

But Cyn was determined to make things right.

One evening, while reviewing old notes in the library, she stumbled across something curious—a name scribbled in the margins of a school directory. It was Xandria's, next to a dorm number that didn't match her current assignment. Intrigued, Cyn dug deeper and discovered that Xandria had been living off-campus for part of the semester, claiming a family emergency. But the truth was more complicated. Xandria had been staying with a distant cousin in town—someone expelled from Thomas-Scott Academy two years ago for hacking into the school's grading system. And now, Cyn had proof that Xandria had been using that same cousin's access to peek at student records, including Mavis.'

Cyn brought the evidence to Mavis, Willow, and Elf. "I didn't know what she was doing," Cyn said. "But I found this. She's been snooping. And not just on us."

Willow's eyes widened. "She's been accessing school files?"

"Looks like it," Elf said, scanning the printouts. "This is serious."

Mavis nodded. "We need to confront her. But we do it together."

The next day, they met Xandria in the courtyard. She was lounging on a bench, flipping through a fashion magazine.

"We know," Mavis said calmly.

Xandria looked up. "Know what?"

"That you've been accessing student records," Elf said. "Using your cousin's credentials."

Xandria's face paled. "You can't prove that."

"We can," Willow said, holding up the printouts. "And if you say one word about our investigation, we'll make sure Headmistress Menard sees these."

Xandria's jaw clenched. "You wouldn't."

"We would," Mavis said. "But we won't—if you keep your mouth shut."

Xandria stood, brushing off her skirt. "Fine. I won't say anything. But don't think this makes us friends."

"No one said it did," Cyn replied, her voice steady. "But maybe it's time you stopped trying to tear people down just because you feel left out."

Xandria didn't respond. She walked away, her silence louder than any insult.

Later that evening, the group gathered in their usual spot behind the greenhouse. The tension had lifted. Cyn sat beside Mavis; her shoulders relaxed for the first time in days.

"I'm sorry," she said again. "I should've known better."

"You learned," Mavis said. "And you helped protect us. That matters."

Willow passed around mugs of cocoa. "To secrets kept—and secrets uncovered."

Elf raised his binoculars. "And to sleuths who stick together."

Chapter 28 – 1127 Wren Hollow Lane

It was finally the weekend—the coveted downtown shopping trip that happened every Saturday, provided you signed up before 3 p.m. Thursday. The shuttle was packed with students tote bags and backpacks, ready to hit boutiques and cafés. But for Mavis and her crew, this wasn't about shopping. It was about sleuthing. Their destination: 1127 Wren Hollow Lane. Dr. York's house.

Backpacks were loaded with essentials. Mavis, ever the walking first aid kit, had packed allergy medicine for Cyn and Willow, napkins for sneezing fits, and aloe for unexpected scrapes. Elf had stocked up at the Gobble-Gobble—the basement eatery in his Oxblood-Gold Dorm—grabbing chocolate bars for the group and chips for Cyn. They were ready.

The plan was simple: don't draw attention. Don't input the address until they were off the shuttle. Blend in. Act normal.

But normal was hard when Xandria was on board. She'd signed up for the trip too, now glued to her new friend Josephine. Her laughter rang out a little too loud, her eyes darting toward Cyn every few minutes. She felt betrayed—Cyn had chosen Mavis and the others. But Cyn didn't care. After discovering Xandria's secret, she knew exactly who she was dealing with.

Blain, the senior who oversaw Mavis' table at meals, was also on the shuttle, sitting two rows ahead. She was friendly, but observant. And then there was Father Trent, the chaperone. He was harmless—more interested in his crossword puzzle than the students.

Still, the group knew they had to be careful.

"I feel like we're in a spy movie," Willow whispered.

"Operation Wren Hollow," Pierson said. "Let's not blow it."

As the shuttle rolled into downtown, the group exchanged glances. Mavis gave a subtle nod. Phones came out, and one by one, they typed in the address: *1127 Wren Hollow Lane.*

They waited until the crowd dispersed—Xandria and Josephine headed toward a boutique, Blain, toward the bookstore. Father Trent lingered near the coffee cart.

"Now," Mavis whispered.

They peeled off in groups—Cyn, Toppy, and Willow towards the art supply store, Elf and Pierson towards the record shop, Franny, Kimp, and Axton towards the bakery. Mavis lingered behind, pretending to tie her shoe, then slipped into a side alley.

One by one, they regrouped two blocks away, behind a mural of a sea turtle wearing sunglasses.

"Everyone accounted for?" Mavis asked.

"Affirmative," Elf said, handing out snacks, they took time packing them in their backpacks.

"Let's find Wren Hollow," Mavis said, her voice steady.

They moved quickly, ducking through side streets and weaving past tourists. The address led them to a quiet lane lined with ivy-covered fences and houses that looked like they belonged in storybooks.

And then they saw it.

1127 Wren Hollow Lane.

A tall, narrow house with blue shutters and a brass knocker shaped like an owl. The curtains were drawn. The mailbox was stuffed. Something about it felt... paused, but still there was a hint of quiet life. It was an anomaly.

"This is it," Mavis said.

They stood in silence for a moment, the weight of their mission settling in.

"Let's find out what Dr. York doesn't want us to know," Willow said.

As they approached the gate, a voice called out.

"May I help you children with something?"

They turned to see a tall, firm man in his mid-seventies, leaning on a carved walking stick. His beard was neatly trimmed, his spectacles looked homemade, and in his other hand he held an unfamiliar instrument—something between a tuning fork and a compass.

"Good morning, Sir," they chorused.

"We're looking for Dr. York," Pierson said. "We're his students."

The man's eyes narrowed, a twitch of suspicion flickering across his features. "Why are you looking for him?"

"We just wanted to visit," Pierson added quickly. "We love his class."

The man pointed at the house. "No one's come looking for anyone there in years. You've made a wasted trip."

His tone shifted—no longer curious, but cold. "Now go along."

They nodded, thanked him, and turned away. But Kimp, sharp-eyed and always scanning, spotted something—a narrow alleyway behind the bakery that curved toward the back of the property.

"I know of another entry," he whispered.

Excitement surged. They regrouped and slipped down the alley, careful not to draw attention. The back of the house was bordered by a high brick wall on either side, but the rear fence was low. They scaled it one by one, landing softly in the overgrown yard.

Willow knelt at the back door, pulled out a slender tool, and picked the lock with practiced ease.

Inside, they huddled in the dark kitchen. Mavis whispered, "No lights. We don't want to alert anyone."

Cyn clung to Elf's arm, trembling. Kimp and Pierson took the lead, followed by Axton, Franny, and Toppy. Willow and Mavis lingered, scanning the kitchen. It was spotless. The counters gleamed. A kettle sat on the stove—and when Willow bumped it, it was still warm.

"This house is lived in," Willow whispered. "Someone's here."

"But who?" Mavis murmured.

Then came the sound.

A creak. A shuffle. From the kitchen they'd just left.

They froze in the living room. Axton spotted a closet and opened it. They squeezed in, breath held, hearts pounding.

"Oh my God, we're going to get expelled," Cyn whispered.

"Nope. I think we're going to get eaten like Hansel and Gretel," Toppy muttered.

"Just stay quiet," Mavis said. "No lights. No movement."

"My arm's falling asleep," Pierson groaned.

"Then let it sleep," Willow hissed.

Footsteps echoed. A tap. A drag. The unmistakable sound of a walking stick.

"The neighbor," Elf mouthed. "But how did he get inside?"

The sound grew distant. Then—slam. A door closed.

Axton was nominated to check. He crept out, scanned the kitchen, then returned.

"There's a door near the fridge. Steps leading down."

Cyn shook her head. "I want to be back on the shuttle. Better yet, back at school."

Elf was calm, focused. "If someone got in once, they could come again. We need to be careful."

They filed down into the basement. It was cool, dry, and surprisingly well-kept. At the far end was another door. Mavis opened it slowly.

A hallway.

Long. Narrow. Lit by faint bulbs strung along the ceiling.

"No," Willow whispered. "It couldn't be..."

"Or could it?" Mavis said. "What if Dr. York's house is connected to the neighbor's?"

They stared into the hallway; the air thick with questions.

Who was the man with the walking stick? Why was the stove warm? And what secrets lay at the end of that hallway? The hallway stretched before them like a tunnel into another world—dimly lit, narrow, and lined with old stone. The air was cool and smelled faintly of cedar and something metallic. They moved slowly; their footsteps muffled against the worn floorboards. At the end of the hall, a door stood slightly ajar. Through the crack, voices drifted out—low, deliberate, unmistakable.

"...students came by to see Sphinx," said one voice. "But I told them no one's come to visit in three years."

"Good, we don't need them or anyone snooping around." Said the other voice. "I wonder who they were?" He continued.

"A group of young'uns."

"Hmm!" He replied.

They froze.

"That's Father Trent," Cyn whispered, eyes wide. "Oh my goodness... Father Trent."

Willow's jaw dropped. "We are definitely in deep dog do-do."

They had suspected others—Menard, maybe even Dean French—but not Father Trent. Reverent, kind, crossword-loving Father Trent. He had always seemed oblivious, harmless. But now....

"If we don't solve this soon," Willow hissed, "and keep anyone from suspecting it's us, we're toast."

"Let's go back," Pierson said. "We need to work fast. Cyn, you're lookout."

"Nope. Not me. I'm too nervous. Pick Axton."

"Me? Why me?" Axton whined.

The group stared at him.

"Fine," he sighed. "I'll risk my life for a good cause."

"So dramatic," Willow muttered.

Toppy was nervous, but curiosity tugged at her. What if Dr. York was being held hostage? What if he was locked in the attic, or worse?

They shuffled quickly back through the hallway and into Dr. York's house. Axton took his post at the secret door near the fridge while the others split up, each assigned a room. They agreed to text if they found anything.

Then—*crash.*

Axton jumped. Everyone scrambled toward the sound.

Pierson had fallen through a weak patch in the floor. He waved sheepishly from below, scraped but intact.

"Oh my God, I saw my life flash before my eyes," Toppy gasped.

"Are you trying to get us caught?" Willow screeched.

Mavis helped Pierson up through the secret side door, cleaning his scrape with water from the kitchen and applying aloe and a band-aid from her ever-ready kit.

"So far, nothing," she said. "This house is hiding something, but where is it?

We need to get back to the shuttle. I think the clock in the furnace at school is our next lead."

Just then, Axton crouched near the refrigerator. "Wait... something's poking out."

He pulled out a folded paper. Pierson snatched it and unfolded it.

"It's a medical bill," he said. "Dated last week."

"Do you think Dr. York is sick. In a hospital?" Willow asked.

"That makes no sense," Toppy scoffed. "He's been gone for four years and teaching as a hologram?"

"Actually," Cyn said slowly, "it could make sense. Maybe he's in a special facility. He's a scientist—maybe he's operating the hologram remotely."

Mavis nodded. "This bill could be the key. If we find the hospital, we might find him."

"We'll need access," Pierson said. "Axton, you're good at hacking."

"School computers, sure," Axton said. "But this might be bigger. We might need help."

"Hey, why not ask Xandria?" he added.

Willow spun around. "Are you nuts? We don't want her anywhere near this."

"She's good at this stuff," Axton said. "She could crack it in minutes."

"She'd also sell us out in seconds," Mavis said. "We can't risk it."

They stood in silence, the weight of the discovery pressing down.

A medical bill. A secret hallway. Father Trent's voice. And a house that looked abandoned but wasn't.

The mystery was deepening. And they were in it—together.

"I'm calling Uncle Adrian," Mavis said, her voice steady but urgent. "It's time we loop him in."

Cyn exhaled like she'd been holding her breath for hours. She didn't want to be the party pooper she'd been labeled, but maybe—just maybe—it was time for a professional. She whispered a silent thank-you to the heavens.

"Do you think he'll have time to look into this?" Willow asked, her brows furrowed.

"Absolutely. I'll call him once we're back at the dorm," Mavis replied.

"Uh... how exactly are we getting out?" Kimp asked, glancing toward the hallway. "Father Trent's next door. Won't he see us?"

"Good point," Pierson added. "For all we know, he's still lurking."

"Guys," Toppy said, squinting toward the neighbor's window, "has anyone noticed the resemblance? The glasses, the eyes... he looks like Dr. York."

"Hmm," Elf murmured. "You know, they do look alike. But everyone has a twin, right?"

"Not me," Willow said with a proud toss of her hair. "I'm one of a kind."

"Except for you, Willow," Elf teased. "But allegedly, the rest of us do."

"Can we stay on topic?" Kimp snapped. "How do we get back to the shuttle without being seen?"

"The same way we came in," Mavis said. "We weren't spotted then—why would leaving be any different?"

"Because Father Trent wasn't next door before," Cyn replied, her voice tight with worry.

"I say one of us checks the tunnel," Willow suggested. "If he's still there, we run. If he's not—"

"We still run," Mavis finished. "We can't stay here. We need to get back to campus."

Cyn made the sign of the cross, her fingers trembling.

"We'll be fine," Mavis assured her. "No bad vibes."

"Yeah, Cyn," Kimp added. "Keep the energy clean."

"I'm not bringing bad vibes," Cyn muttered. "I just don't want us expelled."

"I'll go," Pierson volunteered. "I'm the fastest. If I need to run, I will. Keep the kitchen door open and listen for me."

He slipped down the stairs like a shadow, every creak of the floorboards echoing louder than it should. The group huddled near the door, Axton stationed at the back, eyes locked on the exit.

Silence.

Pierson reached the neighbor's side of the tunnel. Not a peep. Not a whisper. It was eerily quiet—like the house itself was holding its breath. Then, footsteps. Fast. Light. Pierson reappeared, breathless.

"No sound. It's like... like no one was ever there."

Mavis turned to Cyn; her expression unreadable. "I'll go first. I'll text you once I'm over the fence. Willow, you relay the message."

"Are you sure?" Elf asked, stepping forward. "I'm coming with you. You're not doing this alone."

"Me too," said Toppy.

"We all go," Cyn declared. "I may be scared, but I'd rather face trouble together than let you take the fall alone."

Mavis looked at each of them—her team, her tribe. "Are you sure?"

"We're a team," Axton said, his voice firm.

Mavis nodded. "Then we move. Same plan as before—split up, meet at the shuttle. Let's go."

And just like that, the group vanished into the evening, hearts pounding, secrets swirling, and the mystery of Dr. York growing darker with every step.

The students lined up in silence, the late afternoon sun casting long shadows across the cracked pavement. The shuttle idled at the curb, its engine humming like a warning. Father Trent stood at the front of the line, clipboard in hand, his smile stretched wide—but his eyes told a different story. They were sharp. Knowing. Investigative. Each student felt it as they passed him, one by one. The weight of his gaze. The silent judgment. The unspoken question: *Were you the ones snooping around Dr. York's house?* But he said nothing. Just checked off their names with a flick of his pen, nodding politely as they boarded. Inside the shuttle, the tension was thick. No one spoke until they were halfway back to campus, and even then, it was only whispers.

Later, in the safety of Mavis and Cyn's room, the group huddled together. The door was locked. The blinds drawn. Mavis dialed her uncle, placing the call on speaker—low enough that only they could hear. Uncle Adrian had just returned from walking his two Cane Corso's. His voice was calm, gravelly, and curious.

"You've got quite the case on your hands," he said after listening to everything—the hologram, the pocket watch, the medical bill, the eerie silence at Wren Hollow.

"I don't want us expelled," Mavis said quietly. "But something's not right."

"I agree," he replied. "But for now, lay low. No sleuthing. Let me do some digging on my end."

They nodded, even Cyn, who looked visibly relieved.

"There's a centennial celebration coming up, isn't there?" he asked. "Your mum forwarded me the alumni email—rides, roller coasters, a big dance, and a banquet to close the year. Sounds like fun."

Mavis smiled faintly. "Yeah. It's all happening in the coming weeks."

"Good. Enjoy it. You and your friends deserve a break. And stay away from that antique and pawn shop for now. I'll be in touch when I have something solid." Before hanging up, he added, "I'm proud of you, Madison. All of you. You've uncovered more than most trained investigators would. Consider yourselves honourary detectives."

The room erupted in quiet grins and exchanged glances. For the first time in days, the tension eased. But a secret still pulsed beneath the surface. And the mystery of Dr. York was far from over.

Chapter 29 – The Tiara

"Did y'all read that the centennial school dance is this Friday?" Franny announced, flopping onto her bed in Davis-Greene. "Not the formal one—just a casual mixer with Jaxton Morris High."

Mavis, Cyn, Willow, and Toppy looked up from their snacks and magazines.

"I love dancing!" Willow squealed, springing to her feet and twirling in place. Her socks slid on the hardwood floor, making her spin like a top.

The others burst into giggles.

"I don't want to dance," Cyn muttered, pulling her knees to her chest.

Franny tilted her head. "Don't you like dancing?"

"Yeah… just not with boys," Cyn admitted, her voice barely above a whisper.

Willow stopped mid-spin. "We're not dancing with boys. Just with each other—and Elf, Axton, Pierson, and Kimp. You know, the usual crew."

Cyn shrugged. "Well, if it is just us then okay."

Without hesitation, Willow reached for her hand. "Then we'll dance now. No pressure, no music—just us."

She tugged Cyn up, and the two began swaying in a silly, offbeat rhythm. Laughter filled the room like sunlight through the curtains.

"We *have* to find cute outfits," Toppy said, clapping her hands. "Are they taking us downtown again, like last October?"

Franny grabbed her phone and scrolled through her inbox. "Y'all missed the email—it says we've got a shopping trip this Wednesday. But we have to sign up by tomorrow."

"Perfect!" Mavis said. "We can find something for this dance *and* the formal."

"I love a reason to dress up," Franny declared, leaping off the bed. "I want to look like a princess. Well—I *am* Princess Francis." She curtsied dramatically.

Mavis grinned and texted Elf.

Mavis: *We're going shopping tomorrow for the dance. Are you all going too?*

Elf: *I'll ask Pierson. Kimp and Axton said yes. Pierson's in the laundry room.*

Mavis: *Okay, we're all going. Don't forget to sign up.*

Toppy pointed toward the top of Franny's closet. "What's in that green velvet box?"

"Oh, that?" Franny said, reaching up. "That's my tiara and sash."

"You have a *tiara*?" Willow gasped.

Franny opened the box with a flourish, revealing a delicate rhinestone crown and a beige-and-green sash. "I was Little Miss Sapodilla County." She handed the tiara to Willow. "Put it on."

Willow placed it on her head, and Franny passed her a gold hand mirror. "You look so pretty," she said.

"I'd make a pretty princess," Willow beamed.

"May I wear it next?" Toppy asked.

"Of course! Everyone gets a turn. Wait—let me take pictures!"

They posed one by one, striking regal stances and blowing kisses to an imaginary court. Cyn even cracked a smile as she adjusted the tiara on her head.

"Thanks for letting us wear it," she said, handing it back to Franny.

"Anytime. Now let's go sign up for the bus. The sheet's in the office foyer."

They left the dorm in a flurry of chatter and excitement. Blain passed them on the way in, waving casually. Xandria and Josephine had just signed up too. Xandria gave Cyn a polite nod and smirked at Mavis, who didn't flinch. Nothing was going to ruin this day.

Wednesday: Shopping Day

Classes dragged like molasses. By the time the final bell rang, the girls were already halfway to the office. The bus idled outside, its engine humming with anticipation.

Cyn dashed back upstairs—she'd forgotten her purse.

"I'll save your seat!" Mavis called after her.

Cyn returned just in time, breathless, as the driver's hand hovered over the door lever.

"What took you so long?" Mavis whispered.

"My purse was in the nightstand, not the top drawer. I *always* put it in the top drawer."

Willow and Pierson were already seated, chatting. Toppy and Franny giggled nonstop. Xandria and Josephine sat behind them, whispering. Blain and her crew had claimed the entire right side of the bus. Ms. French and Father Trent sat up front, reviewing the itinerary.

Elf and Pierson were deep in conversation. Kimp sat beside Vy, the exchange student from Ghana, who was showing him photos of her family. Axton had earbuds in, listening to a podcast about snake molting.

"I have gum. Want a stick?" Willow offered Pierson.

He shook his head. "Nah. Gum gets boring. Just chewing and chewing and chewing."

Willow shrugged. "Just being polite."

"So... do you think Madison's uncle will get back to us about the York thing?" Pierson asked.

Willow shrugged. "Madison says he will. But honestly, I'm glad we're taking a break. Picking locks was fun, but the whole Dr. York thing gives me the stripes."

"The what?"

"The stripes. It makes me feel uneasy."

Pierson raised an eyebrow. "And you call it *the stripes*?"

"I don't know where I got it from. But yeah. I'm ready for fun."

"Same. Can you believe our first year's almost over? I was so anxious before school started," Pierson said. "I didn't know if I'd make friends or survive the workload. But now? This place feels like home."

"Why did you come here?" Willow asked.

"It was my choice. In my family, we all go to boarding school in seventh grade. My parents think it builds character."

She nodded. "I have been in boarding school from I was little, so this is normal for me. I love making new friends being the youngest with adult siblings."

"Wow, adult siblings?" He remarked.

"Yes, I am from my dad's second marriage, just little me. My siblings are in their thirties."

"Whoa, that is an age gap for sure. Well you have us."

"And I am so happy. You all are my best friends yet."
"We are family." He said.
"Yes, family."

Downtown: The Adventure Begins

The bus pulled up to the plaza, and the students poured out like popcorn. The air smelled of cinnamon rolls and new shoes. Storefronts gleamed with spring displays—sequined dresses, pastel blazers, and mannequins in bowties.

"Let's start at Lila's Boutique!" Franny shouted, dragging Toppy by the wrist.

Willow and Cyn headed toward a vintage shop with velvet curtains and racks of tulle. Mavis lingered by a window display of glittery sneakers.

Inside, the girls tried on everything—ruffled skirts, off-shoulder tops, sparkly headbands. Franny modeled a lavender jumpsuit and twirled like she was on a runway. Cyn found a soft green dress with flutter sleeves that made her feel like she could fly.

Willow discovered a pair of silver boots that made her feel like a disco queen. "These are *so* me," she declared.

Mavis found a teal and orange dress, it was fun, the beige tulle peeping at the hem. She loved it immediately. It would go well with her glitter orange high top sneakers.

They regrouped at the checkout, arms full of bargain finds, cheeks flushed with laughter.

"I can't wait for Friday," Cyn said, her voice light. "Me neither," Mavis replied. "It's going to be magic."

Chapter 30 - The Foyer Before the Fun

The foyer outside the auditorium buzzed with nervous energy. Mavis, Cyn, Willow, Toppy, and Franny stood in a loose circle, each dressed in their carefully chosen outfits from Wednesday's shopping trip. Bouncing tulle skirts, glittery sneakers, gold ballet flats, and awkwardness lingered in the air like a promise.

Inside the auditorium, music pulsed faintly—something upbeat, with a bassline that made the floor vibrate. The students from Jaxton Morris High were already there, clustered near the refreshment table or swaying to the rhythm in small groups. Their voices echoed, deeper and louder than the ones in the foyer.

"I feel like we're waiting to be summoned," Cyn whispered, clutching Mavis' hand like a lifeline.

"We *are*," Franny said. "This is the prelude. The foyer of fate."

Willow giggled. "You sound like Ms. Petty."

Speaking of which—Ms. Petty appeared at the top of the stairs, her rounded afro perfectly shaped, her emerald blouse tucked into a high-waisted skirt that flared just enough to suggest elegance. She waved warmly at the girls before joining the other chaperoning teachers near the entrance.

Headmistress Menard stood beside her husband; both dressed in formal evening attire. Deputy Headmaster Ying adjusted his bowtie while chatting with Dean French and her husband. Father Trent offered a quiet smile to each student who passed, his hands folded behind his back like a benevolent guardian.

The younger students lingered, hesitant. Seventh and eighth graders like Mavis and her crew clung to the edges of the foyer, unsure whether to enter or wait for a cue. The upperclassmen, meanwhile, had already claimed the dance floor—laughing, spinning, and pairing off with ease. Their confidence was magnetic, intimidating.

"I don't know how to walk in there," Toppy murmured. "It's like crossing into another world."

"You just walk," Mavis said, though her voice betrayed her own nerves.

Willow peeked through the double doors. "They have fruit salad. And finger sandwiches. And juice in little glass cups."

"That's fancy," Franny said. "I want a sandwich. But I don't want to look like I came just for the food."

"You *did* come just for the food," Cyn teased.

They laughed, but the tension lingered. The music shifted to something slower, more melodic. A couple of seniors twirled under the soft lights, their movements graceful and practiced.

"Okay," Mavis said, straightening her shoulders. "Let's go in together. Like a unit."

"Like a royal procession," Franny added.

"Like a girl gang," Willow grinned.

They stepped through the doors, the foyer behind them, the dance ahead. The lights dimmed slightly as they entered, casting a warm glow over the room. The scent of citrus and cucumber sandwiches mingled with the faint perfume of the older girls.

Ms. Petty caught Mavis' eye and gave her a subtle thumbs-up.

The girls found a table near the edge of the dance floor, close enough to watch but far enough to feel safe. They sipped juice, nibbled fruit, and whispered about who looked cute, who looked nervous, and who might ask someone to dance.

Leaning in close, Mavis whispered, "I didn't know Headmistress Menard was *married*."

"Me neither," Pierson replied, eyes wide. "She seems so... boring. To be married."

Mavis snorted. "*Boring?*"

"Yes! She's strict and no fun. Who would marry her?" He tilted his head toward the front of the room where Headmistress Menard stood, her posture as upright as ever—until her husband leaned in and whispered something that made her laugh. Actually *laugh.*

"I think her husband is handsome," Toppy said, adjusting the rhinestone clip in her hair.

"He is," Willow agreed, watching them. "And look—he makes her laugh. She *never* laughs with us. Wait... has she *ever* laughed with us?"

Axton chimed in, mimicking her clipped tone: "*Boys to the right, girls to the left. No loitering in the corridor. No gum chewing in chapel.*"

They all cracked up.

"And don't forget," Mavis added, putting on her best Menard impression, "*Mavis E. Madison Jr., take that hideous beaded necklace off at once!*"

She laughed at herself, remembering the sting of being called out for wearing her grandmother's tamarind-seed necklace.

"Oh yes," Cyn said, eyes wide. "I was *so* nervous when she shouted your name across the auditorium. I thought you were going to cry."

"I almost did," Mavis admitted with a grin. "But I didn't want to give her the satisfaction."

Just then, Blain appeared behind Axton like a gust of glittery wind. "Come *on*, you guys," she said, hands on her hips. "You huddle like this at every event. This is a *dance*. Mingle. Move. Live a little."

"We're good here," Cyn replied, clutching her cup of juice like a shield.

Blain wasn't having it. "Willow, I see those shoulders swaying. Franny, you've got that sparkle in your eye. And Madison—don't think I didn't notice you tapping your foot. You look like a dancer."

Before anyone could protest, she grabbed Axton by the wrist.

His tightened in terror. "Wait—what's happening?"

"You're dancing with *me*," Blain declared, already pulling him to his feet. "No escape."

He looked like he'd just been told he had to wrestle a bear in front of the whole school.

The others exchanged glances. Willow shrugged. "Well, she's not wrong."

Franny giggled. "Let's go."

Toppy tossed her curls. "We *did* dress up for this."

And just like that, the trio followed Blain onto the dance floor, swept up in the rhythm of a fast-paced pop song. The lights flickered in time with the beat, casting rainbow glows across the polished floor. Franny twirled like she was on stage, Willow bounced with joy, and even Toppy—usually the most reserved—let loose with a shimmy that made them all cheer.

"This is *fun*," Franny shouted over the music, her cheeks flushed.

Back at the table, Mavis, Cyn, and Pierson watched the scene unfold.

"Should we...?" Mavis began.

Cyn shook her head. "Let them warm up the floor. I'm not ready to be dragged like Axton."

Then she heard it coming up the rear of the speakers, then full boom, "Oh my God, it is Michael Jackson's Thriller." Mavis shouted, like a shock of lightening hit her feet, she jumped up.

Axton joining her, Cyn sitting and tapping her feet.

"Come on Cyn." She then giggled and joined them. Mavis was moving like she was in the Thriller video.

Chapter 31 - The Furnace and the Flicker

The dance was in full swing. Franny had made fast friends with two students from Jaxton Morris High, their laughter blending with the music as they spun across the floor. Cyn lingered near the refreshment table, nibbling a finger sandwich and watching Xandria dance with surprising joy. She glanced toward the foyer, wondering when Mavis, Willow, and Elf would return.

Meanwhile, Mavis and Willow skipped down the hallway toward the bathrooms, their feet pounding like drumbeats. Elf trailed behind, hands in his pockets, humming to himself. At the fork, he veered into the boys' room while the girls disappeared behind the door marked with a swan.

"Tonight is *so* much fun," Willow said, fluffing her curls in the mirror.

"It is," Mavis replied.

"This is my first dance. At my last boarding school, we were too young for this kind of thing. We had movie nights with other schools, and field trips. Those were nice, but this... this is different." Said Willow.

They exited the bathroom together, Elf rejoining them just as the hallway lights flickered—once, twice—and then blazed into a spotlight that seemed to shine directly on them.

Willow froze. "That's... weird."

Mavis tilted her head, curiously.

Elf shrugged. "Probably just old wiring."

But as they turned toward the auditorium, something shifted. The air felt heavier. The lights leading back to the dance flickered erratically, while the corridor toward the furnace room glowed with an eerie, inviting brightness.

"Strange," Mavis murmured. "The way to the furnace is... brighter."

"I know," Elf said. "It's like it *wants* us to come down."

Willow hesitated. "Your uncle told us to wait for instructions. No sleuthing."

"I know," Mavis said. "But a little peek won't hurt. I just want to see if anything's changed with Dr. York's pocket watch."

Willow sighed. "I know this will be trouble. But I can't let you go alone."

"I'm in," Elf added.

They descended the stairs, the hum of the dance fading behind them. The furnace room was quiet, the tall machine still standing like a sentinel. Its soft blue light flickered gently, and the pocket watch nestled in its core ticked steadily—like a heartbeat.

"No voice this time," Mavis whispered. "Just the pocket watch."

"My mother would be furious if she knew I was down here," she added.

"So would mine," Willow said, stepping closer.

Elf circled the machine, eyes scanning for changes. None of them noticed when their left hands, almost instinctively, rested against the metal surface.

Then—everything shifted.

The auditorium was empty.

No music. No lights. Just the echo of their footsteps and the faint murmur of voices—distant, like a memory trying to surface.

Mavis, Willow, and Elf stood frozen in the center of the room, their hands still tingling from the machine's pull.

"This isn't the dance," Willow whispered.

"No," Mavis said, her voice hollow. "This is... something else."

They moved unseen, unnoticed, as people passed them in the hallway of the auditorium at Thomas Scott Academy, Autumn 1929. Shadows of time long gone.

They stood still, watching as frames unfolded before their eyes—like scenes from a silent film. The school was different then. Quieter. Stricter. Cloaked in the scent of coal fires and ink. The halls echoed with the click of leather shoes and the rustle of wool skirts. Discipline hung in the air like dust. The chemistry lab was the crown jewel of the east wing, ruled by the formidable Mrs. Brynn—a woman of precision, principle, and presence. Her reputation preceded her. Her students revered her. And her daughter, Maeve, walked in her shadow. Her daughter, Maeve Brynn, was brilliant. Restless. And drawn to the forbidden. Miriam Langston, her roommate and closest friend, was the quieter one—thoughtful, poetic, and fiercely loyal. Together, they were inseparable. And together, they made a mistake that would echo for nearly a century.

It began in the archives.

Maeve had stolen the brass key from her mother's desk. She said it was for research—something about early alchemical texts and the school's founding. But Miriam knew it was more than that. They crept into the basement late one evening, lantern in hand, the air thick with dust and secrets. The archives were lined with scrolls, ledgers, and relics from the school's earliest days. And in a locked chest, beneath a velvet cloth, they found it: A pocket watch.

It was unlike any they'd seen—etched with symbols that shimmered faintly in the lantern light. The second hand ticked backward. The casing was warm, as if it had a pulse.

Maeve reached for it.

"Miriam," she whispered, "do you feel that?"

Miriam nodded. "It's... humming."

They turned it over. Inside the lid was an inscription:

Time is not a line. It is a knot. Do not pull.

Maeve laughed. "They always say that. Don't touch. Don't explore. Don't *live*."

And she pulled.

The room shifted.

The lantern flickered. The walls rippled. And for a moment, everything was silent—too silent.

Then came the voices.

Not from the hallway. Not from the present.

From *other years*.

They saw flashes—students in different uniforms, teachers they didn't recognize, events that hadn't happened yet. The watch pulsed in Maeve's hand, and Miriam screamed.

Mrs. Brynn burst into the room moments later, her face pale. "What have you done?" she cried.

Maeve dropped the watch. Miriam backed away. But it was too late.

Time had been disturbed.

The Consequence

Mrs. Brynn tried to contain it. She locked the watch away. She warned the headmaster. But the damage had been done.

Miriam began to change.

She stopped aging.

She repeated senior year—again and again. Sometimes in the same decade. Sometimes not. Her memories blurred. Her friendships faded. But Maeve... Maeve disappeared.

Some said she was expelled. Others said she vanished entirely.

Miriam never spoke of it.

No one called her "mum" yet

They turned slowly. The banners on the wall read *Thomas Scott Academy – Class of 1991*. The colors were faded, the fonts blocky and bold. The air smelled of chalk dust, floor polish, and something faintly metallic—like old cassette tape ribbon.

A bell rang in the distance. Not the soft digital chime they were used to, but a loud, clanging bell that echoed through the halls like a call to assembly.

Mavis' heart thudded. "This is the year my mother was a senior."

They slipped into the hallway, careful not to draw attention. Students passed them in uniforms with outdated crests— pleated skirts, oversized blazers, and high-top sneakers. A girl with Mavis' eyes and posture walked by, laughing with a friend.

"That's her," Mavis whispered. "That's my mum."

She looked so young. So free. Not the composed woman who packed lunches and gave lectures about responsibility. This version of her—*Mavis Evelyn Thomas*—was radiant. Her hair was in a high ponytail with a velvet scrunchie, and she wore a denim jacket covered in enamel pins.

"She doesn't know me," Mavis said, her throat tightening. "She's not a mother yet."

Willow reached for her hand. "Then let's not change anything. Let's just... observe."

They followed at a distance, slipping into the back of the auditorium where a group of seniors had gathered. The room was alive now—dimly lit, with a boom box playing a cassette of Whitney Houston's *I Wanna Dance with Somebody*. A stack of CDs sat beside it, each one the size of a dinner plate – well maybe not a dinner plate, but.... A boxy television on wheels flickered with static in the corner, waiting for someone to adjust the antenna.

Mavis' mother was seated on the edge of the stage, legs swinging, surrounded by friends. One of them was unmistakably Wednesday Eclipse—the future Headmistress Menard. But here, she was laughing, her curls bouncing as she leaned into Mavis' mother with a conspiratorial grin.

"She was *friends* with my mum," Mavis whispered. "Before she became Headmistress Menard."

Willow's eyes widened. "She looks... fun."

"She *was* fun," Elf said. "Look at them."

Menard wore a floral blouse tucked into high-waisted jeans; towering twist haloed by the stage lights. She passed a folded note to Mavis' mother, who read it and burst into laughter.

"I can't believe this," Mavis said. "They were just like us."

The girls on stage teased each other, shared snacks from a paper bag, and debated which teacher had the worst handwriting. A boy walked by with a Walkman clipped to his belt, headphones around his neck. Another student adjusted the boom box, flipping the cassette to the B-side.

The room pulsed with life—music, laughter, and the kind of joy that only comes from being seventeen and invincible.

Mavis stepped closer; her eyes locked on her mother. She watched her throw her head back in laughter, lean into Wednesday, and whisper something that made the whole group erupt.

"She's so... *alive*," Mavis said. "I've never seen her like this."

"She's not a mum yet," Willow said gently. "She's just Mavis Evelyn Thomas. A girl with dreams."

"And Menard," Elf added. "She's not married. Not a headmistress. Just a friend."

"I wonder what happened, I mean she and my mum are not friends now. I have never heard my mum speak of her, even at orientation they did not speak." Mavis remarked, still shocked by the revelation of their friendship.

"Well something happened." Said Willow.

"It had to. Do you think this is why she is so hard on me; is it revenge against my mother?" She wondered.

"Sometimes friendships end." Said Willow, "I am not friends with some of the girls from my last boarding school and we thought we would be friends forever."

Shrugging her shoulder, "I guess so." Mavis remarked, still curious but that will be another mystery for her to unfold. Now it was about Dr. York and his pocket watch.

The three of them stood in silence, absorbing the moment. It was like watching a home movie they were never meant to see—intimate, magical, and impossibly real.

Then the lights flickered again.

The boom box hissed. The television blinked. And the air shifted.

The pocket watch was calling.

Its ticking grew louder—no longer just a rhythm, but a summons. The air around Mavis, Willow, and Elf shimmered, bending like heat waves on asphalt. The auditorium faded, the laughter of 1991 dissolving into static.

Then came the pull.

It wasn't violent, but it was absolute. Like being drawn into a memory that wasn't theirs.

The Mad Scientist

They landed in a lab.

Not a classroom. Not a basement. A *lab*—sleek, humming, alive with energy. Fluorescent lights buzzed overhead. The walls were lined with monitors, cables, and glass cylinders filled with glowing liquid. A digital clock blinked: **March 3, 2018**.

Dr. York stood at the center, still human. His lab coat was crisp, his hair flecked with gray, and his eyes burned with obsession. He scribbled notes furiously on a touchscreen tablet, muttering equations under his breath.

Beside him stood **Miriam**.

She was composed, radiant, and strangely out of place. Her blouse was vintage white with a lace collar; her shoes scuffed like they'd walked through decades. Her posture was regal, but her eyes darted—watching everything, calculating.

"She's from the past," Willow whispered.

Dr. York & the Pocket Watch

"But he doesn't know," Mavis said, her voice hushed. "Miriam and Maeve Brynn were roommates in 1929. They disturbed the pocket watch from the archives. It wasn't supposed to be touched." Mavis read the middle of Maeve Brynn's diary just last week, sharing it with Elf and Cyn when she read it.

"And time hasn't been the same since," Elf added.

They crept behind a row of lab benches, careful not to trigger motion sensors. The machine at the center of the room pulsed—a tall, cylindrical device with a glowing core. Inside it, nestled like a heart, was the pocket watch.

It ticked steadily. Loudly. Like it was keeping time for something more than hours.

Dr. York turned to Miriam. "We're close. The resonance is stabilizing. If we can sync the watch's pulse with the quantum field, we'll be able to fold time—not just observe it."

Miriam's jaw tightened. "You're not listening. The watch isn't a tool—it's a tether. It's already connected to too many timelines. If we push it further, we won't be able to control what comes through."

York waved her off. "We're on the brink of something extraordinary. Time isn't a line—it's a loop. And we're about to prove it."

Mavis' breath caught. "He doesn't understand. He thinks he's in control."

Willow leaned closer. "But Miriam *knows*. She's seen what happens when the loop breaks."

The machine began to hum louder. The watch pulsed in its cradle, casting shadows that didn't match the room's geometry. The walls shimmered. A monitor flickered with images— snapshots of different years: 1929, 1991, 2018, and... 2022.

Miriam stepped back, her hand brushing the edge of the console. Her eyes met the watch—and for a moment, she seemed to see Mavis, Willow, and Elf.

Not through sight. Through time.

"She sees us," Elf whispered.

Miriam's lips parted, but she said nothing. Instead, she turned to York. "If you activate it now, you won't just bend time. You'll *break* it."

York didn't flinch. He pressed a button.

The machine roared.

The watch spun.

And the room began to fracture.

The Spark That Broke Time

Then it happened.

A spark leapt from the machine—sharp, electric, alive—and struck the flask in Dr. York's hand. The reaction was instant yet felt like slow motion. Flames bloomed from the glass, crawling up both of his arms, then along his chest, then the left side of his face as if tracing a roadmap of destruction.

Miriam screamed, lunging for the fire extinguisher mounted on the wall. Foam hissed as she sprayed, but the fire had already done its damage.

Mavis, Elf, and Willow stepped forward instinctively, but Willow grabbed their arms.

"If we help," she whispered urgently, "we change something else. This has to happen."

Dr. York collapsed, writhing on the floor. The room filled with the acrid stench of cooked flesh and singed hair. Miriam knelt beside him, frantic, her voice cracking as she shouted for help.

Footsteps thundered down the corridor.

Headmistress Menard burst into the lab, followed by Deputy Headmaster Ying and Father Trent. They froze at the sight—York on the floor, his body scorched, Miriam sobbing beside him.

Menard's face hardened. She shook her head slowly, her voice low and bitter. "He was warned. Again and again. But he always had something to prove."

Mavis, Elf, and Willow remained hidden, watching the scene unfold like ghosts in the corner of time.

Outside, sirens wailed. The fire engine and ambulance screeched to a halt. Paramedics rushed in, their movements swift and practiced. Father Trent murmured a prayer as they lifted Dr. York onto the stretcher. His eyes were closed, his body limp, but the pain was etched into every line of his face.

Menard turned to Miriam; her tone sharp. "This experiment is shut down. Indefinitely. No more funding. No more risks."

Dr. York & the Pocket Watch

"Miriam," Ying said gently, "we don't blame you. You were an understudy. But this has gone on too long. We can't undo what happened to Dr. York—but we *can* make sure it never happens again."

Father Trent stepped forward, his voice firm. "The pocket watch. It's time we lock it away. Deep in the archives."

Menard nodded. "Remove it, Miriam."

Miriam hesitated, then reached into the machine's core. The watch was still ticking—soft, steady, defiant. She handed it to Father Trent.

"I will put it to its resting place," he said solemnly.

Mavis watched him closely. She had never seen Father Trent like this—so commanding, so resolute. More intimidating than Menard herself.

But something gnawed at her.

Why so much blame on a pocket watch? she thought. *It was the spark that burned York. Not the pocket watch.*

And yet... the watch had always been there. Waiting. Watching. Pulling.

The vault door sealed with a low, resonant thud.

Father Trent stood still for a moment, his hand lingering on the iron handle. The watch now rested on its obsidian pedestal, silent. But the silence wasn't peace—it was containment.

Mavis, Willow, and Elf remained in the shadows of the stairwell, hearts pounding. They hadn't meant to follow him this far. But something about Father Trent—his presence, his certainty—pulled them deeper.

He turned slowly, his eyes meeting theirs.

"You shouldn't be here; you are ahead of your time" he said. But his voice held no reprimand. Only weariness.

"We had to see," Mavis said. "We had to know."

Father Trent studied her. He knew. They had discovered the secret of the pocket watch. Then, with a sigh, he gestured for them to follow.

The chamber beneath the chapel was older than the school itself. Stone walls lined with relics, scrolls, and artifacts that didn't belong to any one century. A tapestry hung near the back—faded gold thread woven into the shape of a watch, surrounded by stars and vines.

Dr. York & the Pocket Watch

"This place," Father Trent said, "was built before Thomas Scott Academy had its name. It was once a cemetery. Then a monastery. Then a sanctuary. Now, Thomas Scott Academy. But always... a keeper of time."

He walked to a shelf and pulled down a leather-bound book. Inside were sketches—of the watch, the furnace, the observatory. Names were listed in looping script: *Maeve Brynn, Miriam Langston, Dr. Sphynx York*, and... *Dyan Trent.*

Willow gasped. "You're in the book."

"I was a student here," he said. "Class of 1975. I found the watch in the archives when I was sixteen. I didn't touch it. But I heard it."

Elf leaned in. "Heard it?"

Father Trent nodded. "It speaks. Not in words. In pulls. In shifts. It calls to those who are curious. Those who are lonely. Those who want to rewrite something."

Mavis' throat tightened. "Did you ever try?"

"No," he said. "But I watched others try. And I became the one who kept the stories. The one who made sure the watch stayed buried."

Willow stepped closer. "Then why did you let Dr. York use it?"

"I didn't," Father Trent said, his voice suddenly sharp. "He found it. He stole it. And he thought he could master it." He turned back to the pedestal. "But time isn't meant to be mastered. It's meant to be remembered."

Mavis looked around the chamber. "How many others are like you?"

Father Trent's eyes darkened. "Too many. Some are echoes. Some are shadows. Some don't even know they're displaced."

"Which one are you?" Elf asked, eyes wide.

"I am none of the above," he said. "I am the keeper."

"The keeper?" Mavis repeated.

"Yes. I keep the watch safe—from doing any more harm."

"What will happen now?" Willow inquired, concerned, "I mean now that you have discovered us here, does it affect time; our time?"

"No, you touched nothing, affected nothing. My talking to you has not changed time. I secured the watch in this time but..."

"But..." she began.

He interrupted, "I know you have the pocket watch. It's the only way you and your friends could be here." He said looking at Mavis.

"Are we in trouble?" Willow asked nervously.

He gave a faint smile. "Not if you return it to me. In your time—not in this one."

They looked at Mavis.

She lowered her gaze. "Fine. I'll return it."

"Is there anything we can do for him in our time?" Willow asked.

"Yes, he's a hologram, he's not real and yet he teaches us chemistry. We all want to know how we can help him. How we can find him."

He smiled, but it didn't reach his eyes. "You cannot help him. No one can. Just leave things as they are. The loop was closed in 2020. And we need it to stay closed. You and your friends will reopen things that must remain sealed."

He closed the book and placed it back on the shelf.

"You three," he said, "have seen too much. But maybe... that's what the watch wanted."

Willow frowned. "What do you mean?"

Father Trent looked at Mavis. "You're not just your mother's daughter. You're the next in the line. The watch doesn't choose randomly. It chooses *legacy*."

They left the vault in silence.

But Mavis knew—Father Trent wasn't just a chaplain. He was a guardian. A witness. A keeper of the knot.

Chapter 32 – The Truth

The morning after the dance felt like a dream—soft around the edges, impossible to hold. Had everything truly happened? The time shifts, the shimmer, the watch?

Mavis lay in bed, staring at the ceiling. Cyn was still fast asleep, her breathing steady. Mavis wondered how Willow and Elf were doing. Was she the only one who felt wrung out—like she'd been tugged between decades and generations? She made the sign of the cross beneath her blanket and whispered her morning prayers. She didn't kneel today. Her body was still, but her mind was exhausted.

Cyn stirred just as Mavis finished her "Amen."

"You got in after lights out," Cyn murmured, voice groggy but alert. "Did Biggertoe see you?"

"No," Mavis replied. "Her lights were off when Willow and I passed her door."

Cyn sat up, concern flickering across her face. "What happened, where did you three go, you didn't return to the dance?"

"You wouldn't believe me if I told you," Mavis added, "but I'm just grateful to be safe and sound in our room."

"What happened?" Cyn asked, now fully awake. "Are you okay? Was it Menard?"

"No," Mavis said softly. "She didn't bother us. I'd rather not talk about it. But we need to solve the mystery—and find Dr. York—before the centennial ball."

Cyn sighed, brushing hair from her face. "It was great while it lasted. But yes... we need to know if he's safe. I just want to go back to being regular students again. No more looking over our shoulders, wondering if we'll get expelled for asking questions we weren't supposed to ask." She paused, then added, "And that antique and pawn shop? Madison, I'm begging you—please don't go back there. That place is cursed."

Mavis rose and walked to the window, gazing out at the towering sapodilla tree. "This is who I am, Cyn. I live for mysteries. I love solving the unknown."

"Then save it for after we graduate," Cyn said, half teasing. "Become a private investigator like your Uncle Adrian."

Mavis turned; eyes wide. "Oh my goodness, thank you for saying that. He left me a voice message—I was supposed to listen to it this morning."

"You think he found something?" Cyn asked, curiosity piqued.

"I know he did," Mavis said. "He wouldn't leave a message that late unless it was important."

"Then let's listen with the others," Cyn suggested.

"Agreed. I'll send a group message. We'll meet in the library—Saturday morning, we'll probably be the only ones there besides the librarian."

"Perfect," Cyn said, hopping out of bed. "I'm going to shower. I won't be long."

"I'll go after you," Mavis replied. "Unless Toppy beats me to it. Let me message everyone now."

After breakfast—devoured like it was going out of style— they gathered in their usual corner of the library. No windows. No distractions. Just the hum of silence and the weight of what they were about to hear. Papers were spread across the table, highlighters uncapped, tension thick in the air. It had become their spot—their war room, their sanctuary.

Mavis unlocked her screen. Uncle Adrian's voice message blinked on the screen.

"I found him. Dr. York isn't gone. He is alive— recovering at a burn rehabilitation center in Eastbrook. The hologram had been a cover, maintained by Father Trent and York's twin brother, Saltur."

They were all a buzzed with Ah's, realizing the reason for the resemblance – the old man with the cane is Dr. York's twin brother.

Mavis stared at the address, her heart thudding. "We're going," she said.

The table went silent.

Willow blinked. "Wait—he's alive?"

Elf leaned forward; eyes wide. "So the hologram was real. But also... not?"

Franny clutched her soda can. "This is like something out of a novel. A real one. Not just our lives."

Toppy whispered, "I knew it. I knew he wasn't gone. I felt it."

Pierson exhaled dramatically. "Okay, but can we talk about how wild this is? A twin brother? A secret rehab center? This is next-level sleuthing."

Kimp nodded slowly. "And Father Trent helped cover it up. That's... intense."

Cyn folded her arms. "I'm glad he's alive. But we need to be careful. This isn't just a mystery anymore—it's a legacy."

Axton tapped the table. "So what's the plan? Do we go there? Today?"

Mavis looked around at her crew—her tribe. "We go. Together. We meet Dr. York. We hear the truth from him. And then... we decide what to do next."

They all nodded, one by one.

The mystery wasn't over. But the truth was finally within reach.

The Burn Center

The waiting room was quiet—sterile, humming with fluorescent light. Mavis, Elf, Willow, Cyn, Franny, Toppy, Axton, Pierson, and Kimp stepped through the glass double doors, hearts pounding in unison. Cyn clutched her Rosary, whispering prayers under her breath. She wasn't taking any chances—if divine intervention could keep them from being expelled, she was all in. Mavis offered to speak on their behalf. At the high reception desk sat a man in his late thirties and two women, all dressed in pale blue scrubs. Mavis approached, the others hovering just behind her like a protective constellation.

"May we see Dr. Sphinx York, please?" she asked, her voice steady but soft, her eyes meeting each of theirs with quiet resolve.

One of the women, seated at the far right, looked up. "And you are?"

Mavis hesitated. "I'm... we're his chemistry students. We just wanted to visit him." Her voice trembled slightly. Elf stepped forward to stand beside her, and the rest followed, forming a united front. They were a unit—always had been.

The three staff members exchanged glances. Then the woman nodded gently and gestured toward a small waiting room tucked behind the vending machines and restrooms. "You can wait in there."

They filed in, nerves prickling.

"Do you think she's calling the police?" Kimp whispered.

"I don't think so," Pierson replied. "We haven't done anything wrong."

"And Madison did say please," Toppy added, trying to lighten the mood.

They sat in a tight circle, whispering, fidgeting, glancing at the door every few seconds. Then the man from the desk appeared.

"Father Trent is on his way," he said. "He asked that you stay here until he arrives." His white shoes squeaked as he disappeared down the hall.

Franny stood abruptly. "We should leave. We can sneak out the way we came. We're going to get expelled."

Mavis remained calm. "I don't think so. We can trust Father Trent."

Willow and Elf nodded in agreement.

"I don't like this, Madison," Cyn said, clutching her Rosary tighter. "I'm scared."

Just then, the door opened again. Father Trent entered, followed by a familiar figure—Dr. York's neighbor. The group exchanged confused glances.

"Children," Father Trent said gently, "why did you come?"

Axton stepped forward; his voice sincere. "We just wanted to see him. And tell him... we love his class."

Father Trent looked at each of them, his gaze lingering on Mavis. There was no reprimand in his eyes—only warmth. "Come," he said. "But you must not be loud. This is a place of healing. Use your best behavior—and your best inside voices."

They nodded in unison.

"This is Dr. York's twin brother, Mr. Saltur York," Father Trent added. "We now know it was you all that came looking for him at the house. I was stumped wondering who it could have been."

Saltur gave a small smile and a nod, then turned to lead them down the corridor to Room 222. Inside, Dr. York sat in a wheelchair by the window, bathed in soft morning light. His hair was fine silver, his beard neatly trimmed. A steel-gray robe draped over his frame, and red velvet slippers—plush and worn—rested on his feet.

Dr. York & the Pocket Watch

He turned slowly; eyes curious but kind.

Dr. York & the Pocket Watch

"Sphinx," Father Trent said, "these are your chemistry students."

Dr. York smiled and wheeled himself forward. The scars on his arms and the left side of his face told the story of fire—of pain endured and survived. The burns traced the path of the flames that had once consumed him, now faded but never forgotten. Mavis stepped forward, heart pounding. Despite everything, his face was familiar—like the yearbook photos she'd studied. Like the hologram that had taught her.

"This is Mavis Evelyn Madison, Jr.," Father Trent introduced.

Dr. York's eyes lit up. "I can see it—from the eyes up. Are you Mavis Evelyn Thomas' daughter? Sister to Patricia and Ethelyn Louise?"

"Yes, Sir," Mavis whispered.

"How are they?" he asked, echoing the same question his hologram had posed on her first day of class.

"They're all doing well."

"I love hearing that," he said, his voice warm. Then he looked at the others. "And I'm glad to meet all of you."

One by one, they stepped forward and introduced themselves. He listened to each name, each voice, with quiet joy.

Father Trent and Saltur exchanged a glance.

"Sphinx," Saltur said, "we're taking you home today. The in-home care has been approved."

Dr. York exhaled, his shoulders relaxing. "I've been waiting for this day for four years."

And now, surrounded by students who had followed the truth across time, he was finally going home.

"Children, I'll take you back," Father Trent said gently. "I have the school van. But first, we'll get Sphinx settled at home."

They were elated. The mystery had been solved. Dr. York was alive—not imprisoned in Menard's basement, not lost to time. They waited at the exit as Father Trent drove the van around to the glass entry doors. Inside, Dr. York and Saltur peeked out, waiting for the moment to wheel him forward. The students chatted in jubilance. Even Cyn, who had clutched her

Rosary in fear, was smiling now. Mavis texted Uncle Adrian with the update, thanking him for everything. Father Trent came around the bend like a speed racer, the van's tires humming against the pavement. The wind from his arrival sent leaves and dust fluttering as he stopped in front of the entryway. An orderly in lime green scrubs wheeled Dr. York out, followed by Saltur, who pulled a trolley stacked with luggage, four years of quiet recovery packed into bags and boxes. Relief was etched across all their faces: Dr. York, Saltur, and Father Trent.

On the drive to Dr. York's home, Father Trent explained everything. The hologram had been a safeguard. The agreement was simple: if they could maintain Dr. York's contract and teach his classes through the hologram, he wouldn't be replaced while he recovered. From his bed, Dr. York had prepared every lesson. Saltur had dressed the hologram in his brother's likeness and uploaded the materials exactly as instructed. It was a seamless collaboration—two brothers, one legacy. Father Trent had served as the bridge, updating the administration, relaying school events, and keeping Dr. York informed. That's how the hologram had known Mavis' family, Father Trent chose her to be part of the memory, knowing that her mother and sisters were once students there. It wasn't magic. It was memory, love, and meticulous care. The students listened, marveling. There were questions—about the machine, about Miriam Langston and Maeve Brynn—but those could wait. For now, they simply promised to visit. Dr. York was delighted.

"We're here," Father Trent announced. "Let's get him settled, then we'll head back to campus." He turned to them, voice firm. "You must never speak of this to anyone. The administration must never know you were involved with the pocket watch or Dr. York. Understood?"

"Yes, Sir," they replied in unison, hearts thudding.

Willow's earlier warning echoed in their minds—they were in 'deep dog do-do.' But they didn't care. They were helping. They carried luggage, a kettle, a favorite teacup, and Dr. York's laptop—his most prized possession, filled with end-of-term materials. Once he was settled, Father Trent and Saltur spoke privately. The students sat with Dr. York in the living room, sharing stories from their first year. He listened; eyes bright. It made him feel alive again. He knew it was time to retire—to read, reflect, garden, and heal. Rehab would strengthen his limbs, and maybe, just maybe, he'd take up salsa dancing again. But for now, it was enough to be home.

They said their farewells, promising to visit in the new school year. And they hoped to see him at the centennial celebration. Back in the van, Mavis handed Father Trent the pocket watch. It was a relief to let it go. She'd wanted it because of her grandfather, a watchmaker. But the watch demanded more than curiosity—it required sacrifice. And Mavis had no desire to be lost between decades like Miriam. She loved her life in the present. She'd intended to give it to Dr. York, but she remembered her promise to Father Trent. He accepted it gratefully, relieved to have it back.

"The loop was closed in 2020," he said. "But you reopened it. And you did so with heart." He glanced at them. "I'll drop you at the back entrance. Meet me at the furnace room. We'll give Miriam Langston the farewell she deserves."

Miriam's Farewell

Back at the furnace room, the CPX-1 machine pulsed softly. Miriam stood beside it, eyes calm, hands folded.

"It's time," Father Trent said.

She smiled at the children, her gaze lingering on Mavis, Willow, and Elf.

The others watched, breathless. It was fascinating, terrifying, and exhilarating. They never imagined this would be their first year at Thomas-Scott Academy—but they wouldn't change a thing. Father Trent placed the pocket watch into the terminal one last time. Miriam laid her hand on the watch, then on her heart. The shimmer faded. She smiled at Mavis, then stepped into the corridor of time—back to 1929. Father Trent carefully removed the watch, placing it in a velvet blue box with a heavy combination lock. Only he knew the code. Unbeknownst to Mavis, it was his intention to one day make her the *Keeper of the Watch*. But until then, it would rest in the archives—guarded, protected, and waiting.

Chapter 33 -The Centennial Ball

Thomas-Scott Academy sparkled. Banners stretched across the ballroom: **1922–2022: A Century of Excellence.** Music swelled. Laughter echoed. Light danced across polished floors and satin gowns. Franny twirled with Axton. Cyn sipped punch. Elf and Willow swayed awkwardly but sweetly near the orchestra. Mavis, Kimp, Toppy, and Pierson wandered the perimeter, marveling at century-old exhibits—photos, artifacts, and handwritten notes from students long gone.

Then Headmistress Menard stepped onto the stage. "Tonight," she began, "we are here to celebrate and to honour a century of excellence. We are also, taking time to recognize one of our dear faculty members — a man who, for forty years, was a force to reckon with among his students at Thomas-Scott Academy. Let us welcome Dr. Sphinx York to the stage." She had once vowed never to see him again. The trouble he'd caused, the secrets he'd kept—it had wounded the school's reputation. But Father Trent had softened her heart.

"He's healed," he'd told her. "He's humbled. And he's offered to retire, so the school can move forward. It's time to forgive. Time to celebrate."

She agreed.

Father Trent wheeled Dr. York onto the stage. Applause thundered.

Dr. York spoke slowly, his voice thick with emotion. "I may be scarred," he said, "but I am whole. I am humbled to be here." His eyes shimmered. "I want to apologize to all I've hurt in the past. And I'm grateful for the years to come—years in which this great school will continue to produce students ready to lead the world." He paused, then smiled. "Thank you to the administration for allowing me to be part of this momentous occasion. One hundred years of excellence. Thank you."

He waved gently. Father Trent wheeled him offstage, his commemorative plaque resting on his lap.

Former students from across the decades—some from the eighties, to present —gathered around him, sharing memories, laughter, and gratitude. Mavis' mother and sisters couldn't make the trip, but the room pulsed with legacy.

It was the end of a school year. The end of a mystery. And the beginning of something new. Mavis stood with her friends—her chosen family. They won't be new students next year. They'd be right at home. And as she rubbed her hands together, eyes gleaming, she whispered to herself: *"Now... what's our next mystery?"*

Her friends pulled her onto the dance floor. They giggled, spun, and celebrated beneath the golden glow of chandeliers. The room pulsed with joy, with history, it had become their second home. Above the crowd, a portrait of Mrs. Wilhemina Thomas-Scott watched from her gilded frame, her son and daughter by her side. Her legacy continues.

And, in the vault beneath the chapel, the pocket watch rests in silence.

But silence is never the end. It is the breath before the next chapter.

About the Author

A. Genea Seymour is a multidimensional storyteller and creative entrepreneur whose work is rooted in heart, legacy, and curiosity. Her debut tween mystery, *Mavis E. Madison, Jr. Mystery*, launches a six-part series filled with time travel, ensemble friendship, and the secrets that keeps the mysteries alive.

With degrees in law and business—and a career spanning banking, legal education, and fiction writing—she blends analytical precision with emotional depth. She writes for readers who crave adventure with meaning and characters who feel like family.

She also writes adult romance, historical fiction, and drama under the pen name **A.G. Seymour,** and law study guides under **Anjanette G. Seymour.** Across every genre, her work explores love, resilience, and reinvention.

She loves hearing from readers. Feel free to reach out at: **agsnovels@gmail.com**. Also, join her mailing list at: www.anjanettegseymour.com